MORTIMER HONOUR

After the death of his grandfather in Africa, Joel returns to Scotland to try and find Julia, the love of his youth, who he has never forgotten. But how will Julia react to his return — especially when she discovers that his grandfather's will stipulates that before he can inherit the farm and the Mortimer Diamond he must marry a Scotswoman within a year?

Books by Beverley Winter
in the Linford Romance Library:

HOUSE ON THE HILL
A TIME TO LOVE
LOVE UNDERCOVER

BEVERLEY WINTER

MORTIMER HONOUR

Complete and Unabridged

LINFORD
Leicester

First published in Great Britain in 2002

First Linford Edition
published 2004

British Library CIP Data

Winter, Beverley
    Mortimer honour.—Large print ed.—
    Linford romance library
    1. Love stories
    2. Large type books
    I. Title
    823.9'2 [F]

ROM
1464939

ISBN 1–84395–164–9

Published by
F. A. Thorpe (Publishing)
Anstey, Leicestershire

Set by Words & Graphics Ltd.
Anstey, Leicestershire
Printed and bound in Great Britain by
T. J. International Ltd., Padstow, Cornwall

This book is printed on acid-free paper

1

Stillness settled over the farm as the last rays of the setting sun drained from the African sky, leaving only the calming solitude of dusk. The old man stirred, clutched at the bed sheet with one blue-veined hand and muttered indistinctly. Tired eyelids fluttered open to reveal dull grey eyes from whose depths the life-force was slowly draining.

'Joel?'

The word was a weak, urgent thread of sound.

'I'm here, Grandfather.'

There was a moment's silent understanding as the young man looked into his grandfather's eyes. His own were just as steely, with the same silver flecks, but they held the sheen of healthy vigour. Patiently he waited. Whatever it was his grandfather had to say would be said in his own good time.

Seth Mortimer had lived his life deliberately, determined and without indulgence. He would die in the same manner.

The sounds of the waning day continued unabated, as though this is what the old man would have wanted; the rattling sounds of the birds in the bushes outside the window; the faint bleating of sheep on the distant plain and the melodious singing of the African staff as they trudged home to their cottages in the compound. Marta, the diminutive African cook, was busy in the kitchen of the whitewashed homestead, clattering her pots and pans.

'The will,' Seth murmured.

'It's all right, Grandfather. I know where it is. Don't concern yourself.'

'Please understand. I had to do it.'

'Of course, Grandfather.'

'A bride . . . you must take a Scottish bride.'

Joel tensed. What was the old man on about? His grandfather knew perfectly well he had no intention of ever marrying again.

'Give her the Mortimer Diamond, Joel.'

Joel's frown became deeper. The Mortimer Diamond? No such thing existed! The old man was beginning to ramble. Sensing his grandson's reluctance, Seth Mortimer gathered his strength.

'It was your grandmother's wish that the diamond must go to a Scotswoman, to right a wrong, an injustice. Promise me, Joel,' he whispered.

Exhausted by the effort, he closed his eyes. A little later he mumbled something unintelligible about, 'Mortimer honour.'

Joel hesitated. It wasn't like his grandfather to be sentimental, but if it would ease his passing any, so be it.

'I promise, Grandfather,' he soothed the dying man.

★　★　★

Joel buried his grandfather in the small, family graveyard halfway up the hill beyond the homestead, laying him to rest beside his late wife, Elizabeth. It was a cold, blustery day in early spring, a day as yet untouched by the intense sunshine of summer.

The small group gathered at the graveside was mainly of farm staff, with one or two elderly friends and the family solicitor, Harley Penright, from the nearest town of Hopeford. Joel invited them back to the house where Marta had prepared tea and copious plates of her special fruit cake, in honour of Old Master Seth, she explained tearfully.

'He always liked my fruit cake,' she told everyone.

Joel thanked her, smiling in order to hide the hard lump which had unex-pectedly lodged itself in his throat. His grandfather had inspired both loyalty and affection in all who had known him, not least his staff, and would be sadly missed in the area where he'd farmed so successfully for over fifty years. On a personal level, too, his grandfather's death would be a difficult loss to sustain. Seth Mortimer had been both mother and father to him since the age of fourteen when he'd been orphaned following a motor accident.

On receiving the news, Seth had hidden his own grief, travelled to Scotland where Joel lived with his parents, and offered the distraught boy a home, taking him back to Dusty Plains to live. It was at his grandfather's knee that Joel had subsequently learned all there was to know about life, love and honour — Mortimer honour.

The wind flung Joel's thick, dark hair across his forehead as the solemn party trudged back to the homestead. His thoughts reverted to his grandfather's dying moments, when for some reason or other the old man had been particularly concerned about the family honour, something about righting a wrong deed done in the past. How could this be? Seth had been the most upright man he'd ever known, a man of his word and a fierce opponent of injustice. And yet he'd made it sound as though the family had something to atone for!

'You'll stay to lunch afterwards?' Joel invited Harley Penright as they approached the veranda.

'Delighted,' he replied. 'The reading of the will shouldn't take long. I should like to be back in Hopeford by dark.'

The solicitor darted Joel a quick, assessing glance, wondering how he would react to the unusual terms of his grandfather's will. He decided that Joel Mortimer, like his grandfather, was an honourable man. Once over the initial shock, the young man would do what was right.

Marta had excelled herself with her chicken stew and dumplings. After the meal she served the two men with coffee, depositing the tray on a small table in the conservatory. It was a pleasant, glass-enclosed room where

Seth Mortimer had spent much of the previous winter in a reclining armchair, gazing out at the haunting beauty of the plains.

The remote wilderness area received very little rainfall, its sweet grasses and the occasional borehole alone sustaining Seth's vast flocks of Merino sheep. Beyond these rather desolate plains, to the South, rose the mountain ranges of the Cape hinterland, while to the North, beyond the wide reaches of the Orange River, were the great diamond fields of the country, including the historic city of Kimberley with its famous Big Hole.

Mindful of the fact that Marta was grieving as much as he was, Joel thanked her for the meal and told her that she might take the afternoon off. The housekeeper shot him an outraged look.

'It's Wednesday. I polish the silver on a Wednesday,' she said, and that was that!

The hint of a grin appeared as Joel

poured the coffee. Marta was a stern little creature of habit, very much in charge of the household, and it would not do to ruffle her feathers. He passed Harley Penright one of his grandmother's delicate china cups, wondering why on earth Marta still insisted on using them. He was a big man with large fingers, and the sturdy pottery mugs from the kitchen would have been so much more practical. Setting his own cup down, he lowered his powerful frame on to the green and white striped sofa.

'Well, Harley, you have my full attention.'

The older man cleared his throat.

'Certainly, certainly.'

He lifted his briefcase, extracted a wad of paper and settled his spectacles more securely on his nose.

'This is the last will and testament of Henry Seth Mortimer of Dusty Plains, made this fourth day of March,' he began.

Joel listened in silence while the

solicitor droned on and the coffee at his elbow grew cold. The words washed over him in a meaningless tide.

'I hereby revoke all former wills, codicils or other testamentary provisions and declare this to be my last will . . . express the wish that . . . devise and bequeath the residue and remainder of my estate . . . pecuniary legacies . . . funeral and testamentary expenses . . . '

'Well, there it is,' Harley finished, glancing at Joel over the rim of his spectacles. 'I daresay it's not exactly to your liking.'

Unable to sit still a moment longer, Joel jumped up and paced to the window. Not to his liking! That was the understatement of the year. Even shock was too mild a word! He needed time to think, time to get his emotions under control. He took a deep breath.

'It's preposterous,' he said, his voice low and furious.

There was a heavy silence, when Harley made a sound in his throat which could have been sympathy.

'What was he thinking of?' Joel asked tightly.

'I assure you, Seth was in perfect command of his faculties when he made this will.'

'I have little doubt of that,' Joel retorted. 'But this is all so unexpected. Why did he not discuss it with me first?'

He knew why, of course. He'd never have agreed to it. He'd have told his grandfather to find another way.

'It's nothing but a deliberate attempt to marry me off,' he finished.

Harley inclined his head.

'I'm afraid it does rather look like it. I suppose he wished to ensure that there were Mortimers here at Dusty Plains for many a year to come, and who can blame him?'

Joel turned around, his face set and his voice determined.

'I have no intention of marrying a woman from Scotland or any other darned country, Harley. And I have every intention of keeping this farm!'

Harley Penright cleared this throat and ventured to offer a word of advice.

'Why not give it some thought, at least? If you adhere to the terms of the will and marry within a year, the farm is yours. Then there is the little matter of the Mortimer Diamond.'

His brow creased in bewilderment.

'But why she has to be Scottish, I simply cannot imagine!'

I can, Joel thought, his jaw tightening in frustration. His grandfather knew perfectly well of the woman Joel had always loved, always would, but there was no going back now.

Joel gazed sightlessly through the window, his thoughts on that dull, Scottish afternoon when he'd first seen her. They'd been children, but that one meeting had changed his life. It was enough to ensure he'd carried her image in his heart all the way to Africa, an image he'd been determined to replace with the real thing once he'd become a man.

For years the ideal had lent fervour

to his studies and purpose to his life. Once he'd obtained his degree, he'd travelled to Britain for post-graduate study, determined to find her again and make her his. But he'd been too late. She'd married another man, albeit one who'd left her within a year despite the knowledge that there was a baby on the way. The fact that she was free again should have had him rejoicing, but it hadn't. He'd been nothing but a proud, blind, stupid fool.

He'd returned to South Africa, determined to forget her. He'd tried to make another life for himself, marrying without thought a pretty girl from Kimberley who'd been after him for years. But it was a big mistake.

Harley Penright coughed nervously.

'Joel?'

He looked up blankly.

'Yes?'

'About the Mortimer Diamond.'

Joel sighed.

'When Grandfather rambled on about it the other day I thought he was hallucinating. What Grandfather said at the time was meaningless to me.'

His steely eyes searched Harley Penright's face as though the answer was written across it in black ink.

'Where the dickens is the thing?'

Harley cast him a look of astonishment.

'You don't know?'

'I wouldn't be asking if I did.'

'No. Well, I'm afraid to tell you that Seth refused, against my advice, I might add, to put it in a bank vault. He insisted on keeping it here at Dusty Plains. I have the combination number of his safe here somewhere. The diamond is extremely valuable, and a little piece of history at that.'

Joel's gaze sharpened.

'History?'

'Certainly. It ranks up there with the Eureka stone, I believe.'

'Good heavens, that was South Africa's first diamond of any importance, discovered 'way back in 1866.'

'Precisely.'

Joel's lips thinned. Why had his grandfather said nothing about such a valuable family gem? It was downright embarrassing.

'Can you give me any more details, Harley?'

'I believe Seth told me it was discovered on the banks of the Orange River by a young Scotswoman. There was quite a to-do about it at the time, some scandal or other.'

'When was this?'

'Oh, towards the end of the nineteenth century, I think. I really cannot recall much of what your grandfather told me. It was a long time ago, Joel, long before you came here.'

'Wasn't that period roughly when the first diamonds were discovered at Kimberley? It marked the start of the whole diamond industry in this country,' Joel mused.

'I daresay. Being a historian, you would know more about it than I do.'

'Just after that came the discovery of gold near Johannesburg,' Joel went on, eyes turned cold, 'and before long the country was inundated with foreign fortune-seekers, the Scotswoman notwithstanding.'

Harley nodded.

'Few can resist an El Dorado in the making, my dear chap.'

'With everyone imaginable out to seek his fortune and then fight over it.'

'Greed is an unfortunate human trait,' Harley agreed, gathering up his documents. 'I wonder who the woman was.'

Joel's voice revealed his disgust.

'I've no idea. She was doubtless just as greedy as the rest of them.'

He wondered yet again why he'd heard nothing of all this before. Did the family have something to hide? What price then, the Mortimer honour?

'All you have to do,' Harley encouraged as he fastened his briefcase, 'is to find this person, marry her, present her with the diamond, and all will be well. That way, the diamond stays in the family and you get the farm. A very neat solution but what escapes me completely is the reason for all of this.'

Joel, not quite sure himself, did not enlighten him.

★ ★ ★

For the next month, Joel continued to argue with himself. He needed to gain some kind of closure to be able to put his grandfather's death behind him. But how could he when so much was at stake? He needed space, he decided, throwing himself into his work. He was not ready to make a decision.

Spring flowers emerged in the flower-beds and the days became warmer. Joel took a break from his work one day and wandered out into the garden. He leaned over the ranch-style fence and contemplated the distant plains with their covering of low, much-branched shrubs so beloved of the sheep which grazed them.

He couldn't ever remember himself not being able to summon the courage for something, except perhaps as a boy when grandfather had caught him stealing the keys of the gun cupboard. He'd thought of lying his way out of the situation, until Grandfather had sat him down and taught him all about honour, Mortimer honour.

'Dinner is served, Master Joel,' Marta's voice broke into his thoughts.

Joel retraced his steps to the large dining-room. The room seemed particularly empty now without his grandfather. He ate his steak as though it were cardboard, so that Marta, arriving with the next course, pursed her lips. Anyone could see that the master was lonely. It was not her place to say it, but what he needed was a good woman to improve his temper.

Joel, oblivious to these homespun homilies, tackled his pineapple sponge without seeing it. Rather than consider the issue which he knew perfectly well he'd been avoiding, he turned his thoughts once more to his work. The rather obscure historical subject his publisher had suggested for his next book needed copious research but for once he just didn't have the stomach for it.

He sipped his coffee and thought about his life at Dusty Plains. It wasn't as though he were cut out for farming, exactly, yet he loved the place and had done from the moment he'd arrived. As far as the farm itself was concerned, he had no cause for complaint. The manager, Piet Driemeyer, who lived with his small family in the cottage over the hill, was the finest farmer you could find. Together with his team of African shepherds, he had everything admirably under control.

The farm remained prosperous and now that spring was here, extra staff would be hired to cope with the lambing. Everything was just fine. But it wasn't his surroundings which bothered him. Outwardly all was ordered and serene, but inside his heart and mind it was a different story. Joel turned his thoughts to something else

— the Mortimer Diamond.

He'd found it tucked away in a black velvet bag in a box in the safe together with its insurance papers, and he'd whistled when he'd seen the figure in black and white. Harley was right. The precious thing ought to be in a bank.

He drained his coffee cup and refilled it from the silver pot Marta had left at his elbow. It would be interesting, he mused, to research the origin of the stone. Its find was important enough to have been documented, and what's more, he had a strange compulsion to discover the name of the woman who'd found it. With the first lightening of his spirits in many days, Joel took himself to bed. The proposed break from his normal routine would help restore his sense of equilibrium and by then he would be in a better frame of mind to tackle the unpalatable decision he knew was still awaiting him — to take a wife, or not to take a wife. Until now he'd always been a man who knew exactly what he wanted. He was not accustomed to these agonies of indecision. What he needed was something mind-blowing to propel him out of this numbing inertia and the restless ache which had plagued him for weeks. He knew its origin, of course, but all thoughts of her had long since become taboo.

2

The damp Scottish weather had been annoying Julia Thornton for weeks. What a foul day it was for a wedding! Couldn't the sun have peeped out just this once?

'I pronounce you man and wife,' the vicar intoned.

She took one look at her younger sister Ginny's ecstatic face and breathed a sigh of relief. A few weeks ago it had been Kirsty's turn at the altar, the other twin, and now they were both off her hands, so to speak. She could relax in the knowledge that there would be no further weddings in the MacGregor family, not ever!

Julia wasn't against weddings, as such. She'd even had one herself, once, followed by the brief, inglorious marriage she'd long since put behind her. It was just that when all was said and done, men weren't all they were cracked up to be!

'You may kiss the bride,' the vicar was now saying.

There was a murmur of approval from the congregation as Tim proceeded to do just that, but Julia scarcely noticed. It all started, she thought glumly, when you sink into a man's arms and then end up with your arms in the sink! Not that she was against housework, or gardening or cooking or motherhood. On the contrary, she enjoyed them all. What's more, she'd been doing all these things for years, since her sixteenth birthday, to be exact.

On that day, her parents had died in a flying accident and her youth had been cruelly snatched away, to be replaced by the terrifying and relentless burden of responsibility she'd shouldered ever since. Now, at last, she would be able to relinquish it, and to be honest, she was glad to. At twenty-seven, she already felt like an old woman.

'Dash!' Julia whispered, glancing down at her pretty pink fingernails.

One of them was broken, the undoubted result of all that last-minute stripping of flowers she'd undertaken in order to assist Mrs Norton, the vicar's wife. She clenched her hands into fists and took a trembling breath. Her nerves were stretched, to say the least! It would be the last straw if anything went wrong at the reception, but judging by all the last-minute mishaps they'd endured, nothing more could possibly go wrong, could it?

After today she could relax.

Did she say relax? How could she relax when Aunt Jemima was coming to stay? And she was bringing her obnoxious godson, recently arrived from South Africa, or rather, he was bringing her, in some fancy motor car, hired with lots of fancy money. Just to make matters worse, she'd had neither the time nor the means this week to restock her freezer.

Her thoughts strayed to Aunt Jemima's godson and all that wealth. According to family rumour the money had been acquired illegally, something to do with diamonds at the turn of the century, or so Aunt Jemima's twin, Aunt Harriet, had once informed her. Twins ran in the MacGregor family, Julia acknowledged.

Not that Julia ever took Aunt Harriet seriously. She was a fountain of gossip, most of it mistaken. All she remembered was that Aunt Jemima's godson had been a hateful boy who had probably grown into a hateful man. How could she ever forget the way he'd teased her about her teeth? And he'd had the gall to laugh outright when she'd attempted to climb the old apple tree in the garden, all eight-year-old clumsiness and awkward puppy fat. Well, she couldn't help being an ungainly child, or having to wear those ugly braces on her teeth, could she?

Determinedly Julia put the scene from her mind as the congregation launched into the final hymn. She prided herself on being able to handle most things which life threw at her these days, and to date there'd been bereavement, responsibility, divorce and financial hardship. So what was a little ridicule into the bargain? What's more, she'd grown into a sleek, well-groomed female with stunning legs and a smile to die for, or so she'd been told. The fact that it had been Carl who'd said it right at the start of their relationship brought a grim set to her mouth.

Deliberately Julia re-examined her broken fingernail. What was she doing? This was no time to be thinking of ex-husbands! Weddings were supposed to be romantic occasions, if you believed in happy-ever-afters, that is. Fortunately, she didn't.

The bridal party was now processing down the aisle.

'Isn't he wonderful, dear?' old Mrs Guthrie, the postmistress, leaned across and whispered.

Julia smiled and nodded. True,

Ginny's doting bridegroom looked almost handsome. It was amazing what a morning suit did for a man! Ginny herself was radiant, which was as it should be, and despite her cynical thoughts, Julia felt a small, irrational pang of envy. She hid her pain behind a brilliant smile. If the truth be told, she'd had enough supposed sentimentality for one day, and as for having to listen to a young man swear undying love, even if it was to her dear sister, Ginny . . . yuk!

'Men,' Julia had informed her image in the mirror that morning, 'haven't the faintest clue what makes a woman happy. Where the opposite sex is concerned, they have the intelligence of hanging beef!'

She'd even argued the case fiercely with her colleague at the doctor's surgery where she worked, Cilla McGuire.

'The more macho a man is, the less he understands how a woman ticks!'

Cilla, collecting up a bundle of files,

had viewed her pityingly.

'But I'd rather have a real man than a wimp, any day. So what if he lacks a little understanding? You can always train him, can't you?'

'That's where you're wrong, Cilla. Men are stubborn. They can only think of two things, money and getting a woman into bed. In my experience,' Julia had insisted, warming to her theme, 'men are ruled by their hormones, or their pockets, or both! And they just don't do commitment. A man's idea of commitment is to write a woman's name in his little book and then forget all about her. And if the creep ever gets as far as marriage, within a year he leaves the little woman and begins making like a tomcat on the prowl.'

'But that's not always true,' Cilla uttered in disbelief.

'The trouble with men is they're utter frauds!'

Julia's voice had held a bitter ring. Her ex-husband had been not only a fraud, but a cad. She'd fallen for his smooth charm and glib line in flattery, and fallen hard, just like a clay pigeon, unaware of the gunfire until it had been too late and her life had been shattered into tiny pieces.

How dumb could a girl get, believing the lies of a man like that? It hadn't taken long to discover that he'd married her in cold blood for his own selfish reasons — to safeguard an inheritance from his crazy father, who'd made an even crazier will, stipulating that his son had to take a wife within a year.

Carl had immediately set about finding one. Almost as soon as he had the ring on her finger, he'd switched back into bachelor mode. He'd enjoyed a variety of other women and even flaunted them in her presence, then stayed just long enough for her to become pregnant. Then he'd taken off for good, secure in the knowledge that his father's money was safely in the bank. Julia's humiliation had been complete, and she'd vowed never to love again.

'Come along, dear,' Mrs Guthrie's voice intruded on Julia's thoughts.

With a start, Julia realised that Ginny and Tim had disappeared through the church door. With her smile determinedly in place, Julia took her small daughter by the hand and nudged her towards the end of the pew.

'I want to throw my rose petals, Mummy,' Meggie whined.

'Hush, darling. Wait until we're outside.'

But Meggie wasn't to be left out of things. She pushed Mrs Guthrie and scuttled between the legs of a fat man in a pin-striped suit — Ginny's boss, Julia realised in dismay. He glared at her and muttered something uncomplimentary about mothers who couldn't control their children.

'So sorry,' Julia murmured in embarrassment.

Ginny and Tim were all smiles as cameras popped and confetti enveloped them in a pastel cloud. Meggie was nowhere to be seen. Julia slipped through the crowd of villagers, her eyes narrowed. Her daughter's persistent cough had kept her awake for most of the previous night and after all the stress of the past weeks she was fast approaching the end of a very short tether. Where on earth was the child?

'Is this what you are looking for?' a masculine voice drawled.

There was a hint of impatience in the deep tones and the words uttered in a slightly foreign accent. Julia spun around and found herself confronted by a vast chest, graced by a neat grey waistcoat under a neat grey suit, and complimenting these sober garments was a pale blue shirt and an expensive silk tie, all of which appeared to belong to a veritable giant.

As her glance travelled upwards she noted a breadth of shoulder seldom seen in man, and a strong, tanned column of throat with a tough-looking jaw. Firm, well-shaped lips were compressed as though in disapproval and narrowed, intent eyes were regarding her warily from a great height. They were breathtaking eyes, steely, almost as dark as his suit, with tiny silver flecks glittering in their depths.

Julia was feminine enough to gape before her usual defence mechanisms kicked in and she favoured the giant with one of her iciest stares. She had become good at icy stares, having taught herself to be coldly dismissive with all male comers-on. Beneath the stare her heart skittered like a panicked colt as the blood galloped through her veins.

If she knew a prayer, Julia thought wildly, now was the time to say it! Or run, because every feminine sense told her this man was more dangerous than a lighted cigarette in a fireworks factory.

'You must be Julia Thornton.'

Her hazel eyes widened. How did he know that? She studied him more closely and found there was something intensely familiar about those magnificent, darkly-lashed eyes.

She gasped in belated recognition.

Good grief! It was none other than Aunt Jemima's godson! The tall, lanky boy she'd known had grown into a large man with a tough, uncompromising manner. He had an air of intense physical power, but although he was an intimidating, sophisticated man, Julia had the impression that he was totally without pretence, unlike Carl had been.

Joel Mortimer watched the flush creep over Julia's cheeks with a certain amount of interest. He wasn't a conceited man but her startled, hurriedly suppressed reaction had been appealing, to say the least. She was even more lovely than he'd remembered, a little thinner, but it suited her, emphasising the delicate beauty of her bone structure. Her glossy dark hair was swept back into a knot severe enough to deter even a bigamist, he noted in secret amusement. And that complexion was still like porcelain. A Celtic rose, if ever there was one, and so vastly different from the tanned, sturdy young woman of his acquaintance.

Conscious that he was staring, he glanced away casually. She'd recognised him! That was something, at least. He thought he'd been prepared for this meeting. He'd even steeled himself for it. But here he was, eyeing her like a dazed owl and feeling as hot as a teenager on his first date.

Julia lifted her chin.

'Yes, that is correct. I'm Julia Thornton.'

Something caught deep inside him. Beneath the defiance she still had that vulnerable air which made him wish to shield her from the rest of the world, not that she'd thank him for doing so, he reflected wryly. As he remembered, she'd been a fiercely-independent little female. Those dark brown eyes had gazed upon him with such admiration one moment, and childish scorn the next. They were startling eyes which hadn't changed, even now, except that there was something added — a hint of sadness, of disillusion, eyes which beckoned a man and held him off at the same time. Irresistible! He took a deep breath and cleared his throat.

'And this little person is?'

'Meggie, my daughter.'

Joel had expected to dislike on sight the product of her marriage to another man, but he'd found the child utterly charming. What Meggie had just said to him had quite taken his breath.

Julia recovered herself enough to regain some remnant of poise. She swallowed hard, aware that a tiny pulse was beating frantically in her temple, the telltale evidence of how deeply his presence was affecting her.

'Julia?'

Hostility crept into her eyes, masking the apprehension.

'Yes?'

She would not allow herself to feel threatened, no matter how overpowering the man was. There was nothing to be afraid of, least of all a macho male regarding her with all the arrogance of someone who knew precisely what effect he was having.

'Wh-what are you doing here?'

Mortified to discover that her voice came out in an alarmed squeak, Julia blushed the colour of her lipstick. It wasn't fair! She wanted to hide under a stone, whilst this creature was so confident you'd think he was bullet proof.

'I'd have thought it was obvious,' he mocked.

He was supposed to give Aunt Jemima a lift but as far as Julia knew he hadn't actually been invited to the wedding, or had he? She hadn't seen the final guest list because that had been Ginny's department. To add to her embarrassment, Julia became aware of her daughter waving with glee at her from her perch high upon the man's shoulder.

'You may put Meggie down, now,' she snapped, adding a rather ungracious, 'Thank you.'

'It would be as well if you watched her more closely. The child came hurtling down the steps and all but landed in the street. She could have been injured by a passing car.'

He swung Meggie down, depositing her at Julia's feet.

'There you are, Mrs Thornton.'

Julia's eyes darkened in anger. It hadn't exactly been her fault that Meggie had run away like that! An unwelcome thought struck her. If he'd known who she was, what else did he know about them?

'Did you bring Aunt Jemima with you?' she asked.

The old lady would stay with her and Meggie in their small, rented cottage but there was absolutely no way she was letting this unspeakable person invade her space, too.

'Naturally,' he replied coolly. 'Did you expect her to use public transport? She's nearly eighty, you know.'

'I am well aware of my aunt's age,' Julia gritted.

As Joel Mortimer gazed at her flushed face, the coolness vanished. The lovely Mrs Thornton looked tired and strained, and for a moment he very much wanted to kiss her.

Instead he observed blandly, 'You know, you'd be breathtaking if you allowed yourself to smile. You're glaring at me as though I were poison.'

Julia gasped. Did the man have no manners? To cover her embarrassment she turned to Meggie.

'It was naughty of you to run away like that,' she chided.

Meggie's mouth trembled.

'The man lifted me up so I could throw my roses, Mummy,' she explained. 'I like him, Mummy. I asked him to be my daddy.'

Julia stole an appalled glance at Joel Mortimer from under her thick fringe of lashes, only to find herself quite unable to read the look on his face.

'Well, thank you for rescuing my daughter,' she offered stiffly. 'I'm sorry she troubled you.'

'Oh, I wouldn't say she was any trouble.'

Joel began a thorough scrutiny of her cream suit and matching straw hat. Julia blushed again, and this time the heat travelled the entire length of her body. She was quite unaware of how appealing she looked. Unable to afford a new outfit for the wedding, she'd searched the charity shops and now had the uneasy feeling he knew exactly how much she'd paid for it! With all that money he was bound to have expensive tastes. He'd consider her clothing woefully inadequate, Julia thought, but see if she cared!

Joel Mortimer appeared to be transfixed by her grandmother's antique pearl brooch. She'd pinned it strategically in the front where her neckline had dipped a little low, quite unconscious of the fact that it actually drew attention to her pretty shape.

His voice roughened.

'I can't say the same for the mother,

unfortunately,' he added.

'What is that supposed to mean?' Julia demanded.

She'd been called many things, but never trouble!

'It means that you're a dangerous woman.'

'You make it sound as though I was part wildcat, part shrew and part she-wolf!' she said indignantly.

Joel's mouth twitched.

'What I meant was, women like you light all kinds of fires, and when a woman plays with fire, it's usually a man who gets burned.'

'You're wrong,' Julia retorted, her eyes flashing sparks. 'It's the man who's the wolf. He deserves all he gets. And this is a ridiculous conversation to be having!'

Without another word she marched Meggie away. Talk about danger! If he had the plague, she couldn't be more terrified. She plunged into the crowd of well-wishers, trying to ignore the disturbing encounter. The man had more sex appeal in his little finger than Carl had in his whole body, and just look where Carl's attractions had got her.

The reception was to be held in the village hall, a few minutes' walk from the church. Julia shivered in the damp, autumn air, wishing she'd brought her winter coat. It was old and shabby, and pride had dictated that she leave it at home, which hadn't been a very sensible thing to do. Meggie, on the other hand, in her red and green MacGregor tartan and new Aran jumper under her padded coat, seemed impervious.

'Do hurry, darling,' Julia cajoled. 'This isn't the time to dawdle.'

But strong-willed little Meggie was in one of her obstinate moods.

'Don't want to,' she declared.

Julia shivered again.

'You want to see Aunt Ginny and Uncle Tim cut the wedding cake, don't you? Come along then.'

'Don't want to,' Meggie began

automatically before pausing to reconsider. 'Will my daddy be there?'

Julia held on to her temper.

'No, darling.'

Meggie knew perfectly well that Carl was no longer with them.

'Your daddy lives far away, remember?'

Like at the opposite side of the globe, and thank goodness for that.

Meggie shook her mop of dark curls and all but dislodged her red bow.

'I'm talking about my new daddy. Will my new daddy be there? The big man with the deep voice and the funny accent and the nice smile. The one who helped me throw my roses, Mummy.'

If Joel Mortimer had been anywhere near at that moment, Julia would have throttled him. It was all his fault that Meggie was playing up, and it was completely unacceptable that the child, young as she was, was fascinated by him, too. Joel Mortimer was a total stranger, and total strangers had no business worming their way into the affections of other peoples' children.

Suppressing her irritation, Julia tugged Meggie along the slippery pavement. Her daughter's desire for a father was becoming a real problem. She'd even taken to informing God in her prayers at night that she would prefer to have a daddy who lived with them, like Jamie's. It was high time for another chat. She would explain to Meggie once and for all that although God always heard our prayers He did what was best for us, and that did not necessarily mean giving us what we wanted. A daddy would more than likely not be forthcoming. One marriage had been enough.

'Will my new daddy be there?' Meggie persisted doggedly.

'If you mean Mister Mortimer, yes, he'll be there,' she said carefully, 'but you have to understand, Meggie, that he is not your father.'

Meggie stopped in the middle of the pavement and stamped her foot.

'Yes, he is! I want him to be.'

Julia sighed. It was no use trying to argue when Meggie was in this kind of mood. How well she remembered the Terrible Two phase, when everything she'd said had been contradicted by a small girl learning to assert herself. Then they'd endured the clingy, Thumb-sucking Three stage, when for some reason she'd refused to let Julia out of her sight. Now it appeared they were going through the Frightful Fours! Perhaps, she thought hopefully, next year would be the Fabulous Fives.

'We're nearly there. Come on, darling,' she coaxed.

But Meggie was gazing raptly down the street. She had spotted the object of her affections and nothing else mattered. Like a small tornado she jerked free and flew down the pavement, flinging her arms about Joel's long, muscular legs as he alighted from a dark blue Mercedes. Startled, he looked down from his great height. Amusement warmed his steely eyes.

'Oh, it's you.'

Without as much as a glance in Julia's direction he tucked Meggie under one arm and steadied Aunt Jemima with the other before shepherding them both into the village hall.

'Well!' Julia exploded.

She might as well have been invisible. The man had high-handedly taken charge just as though he really were Meggie's father! She would make it clear she would not tolerate such interference.

3

The hall was filled with animated guests already seated at round tables which had been tastefully clad in lilac to match the colours of Ginny's bridal party. Some of the guests had already been served with the champagne of modest vintage which Tim had provided, and were preparing to enjoy themselves.

Julia paused to view the impressive floral arrangements, also paid for by Ginny's groom, and considered that all in all they'd done well on their limited budget. Of course, had their parents still been alive, it would have been a different matter entirely. Her father had been a successful barrister.

Once more, Meggie was nowhere to be seen. Julia spotted her aunt seated alone at one of the tables.

'There you are, my dear,' Aunt

Jemima observed, offering one lined cheek to be kissed.

The old lady had been a beauty in her day, and Julia was said to resemble her, a fact of which she was secretly rather proud.

'Virginia makes a splendid bride, does she not?'

'Beautiful,' Julia agreed, adding generously, 'and so did Kirsty.'

She produced a sunny smile which quite failed to deceive her aunt. Unaware that she sounded wistful, she went on.

'I hope Ginny and Tim will be very happy together.'

Aunt Jemima's blue eyes held compassion.

'I'm sure they will be, my dear. Virginia appears to have made a wise choice.'

The words only served to remind Julia what a fool she'd been. The old lady patted the seat beside her.

'Do sit down and tell me how you managed to produce another

marvellous wedding so soon after Kirsten's, my dear.'

Hiding her impatience, Julia looked about her.

'I must find Meggie first. She's disappeared.'

'Oh, I shouldn't worry, dear, she's perfectly safe. She's with my godson.'

Julia clenched her teeth.

'I rather gathered that. Meggie's my daughter and Mister Mortimer had no right to abduct her.'

Aunt Jemima looked taken aback.

'That's a little strong, isn't it? He's merely taken her to find some orange juice, and it's doctor, not mister. He's a world-famous historian you know.'

Julia was unimpressed.

'Whatever. Well, he could have waited for me. What if Meggie had been allergic to orange juice?'

'Nonsense, dear. You're a little strung up, that's all. It's not like you to overreact in this fashion.'

Julia swallowed her frustration. Aunt Jemima was right. She was feeling cross, tired and confused.

'I'm sorry,' she said quietly, and sat down.

'I propose to stay with you and Meggie for the next few days,' Aunt Jemima was saying. 'I hope that will be in order.'

'You are very welcome, Aunt. I only hope you will be comfortable enough in such a tiny cottage.'

Once more Julia thought of her empty freezer. It would have to be omelettes for supper.

'Joel will drive me back to Little Crawford on Wednesday, of course.'

Julia made a mental note to be out when Aunt Jemima's godson arrived. She felt compelled to clarify matters.

'I presume he has somewhere to stay?' she enquired hastily.

'Oh, yes. He's putting up for a night or two in the village before going on to Edinburgh to look up some old South African friends. Then I believe he'll be chasing around the country on a lecture tour before going home.'

Julia tried not to be too curious.

'Where's home?'

'He lives on a vast sheep farm in a remote part of South Africa. Did you not know?'

'No.'

For no reason at all Julia felt deflated. South Africa was on the other side of the world! Telling herself sternly that the less she and Meggie knew about the handsome historian, the better, Julia stifled any further questions and began to chatter about the wedding. But it appeared that Aunt Jemima wasn't about to let the subject drop. Her blue eyes grew thoughtful.

'Joel informs me that he spoke to you outside the church, Julia.'

'Yes, I believe he did.'

'He seems to consider you to be a rather prickly young woman,' her aunt said, sounding puzzled. 'He said you were as pretty as a June rose but possessed all the thorns in creation. He couldn't get near for fear of being cut to shreds.'

She ignored Julia's look of outrage and continued.

'I told him not to be misled, that you were a lovely girl, but like some of those special South African chocolates he brings me, you had become rather dark and bitter on the outside, with a sweet, soft centre, of course,' she amended.

Unable to think of a suitable reply, Julia glared at the pretty floral centre-piece on the table. Is that how everyone saw her? Had she allowed her life experiences to make her bitter and twisted? Suddenly, Meggie appeared at her side, clutching Joel Mortimer by the hand, her small world blissfully complete.

'My daddy and I fetched me some juice,' she informed everyone triumphantly.

Thankfully, Joel appeared not to have heard. He placed a large glass of orange juice on the table and calmly offered Meggie a chair next to Aunt Jemima. Agitated, Julia jumped up.

'We can't stay. I must find another

table. Come with me, Meggie.'

Pigs would fly before she'd spend any more time in Joel Mortimer's company. This was her sister's wedding, and she intended to extract what little enjoyment she could from the afternoon, for goodness' sake! But Meggie's mouth turned down at the edges.

'I want to sit next to my daddy,' she insisted then turned to Aunt Jemima and informed her proudly, 'Mummy bought me this new jumper for the wedding, and I'm wearing the Mac-Gregor tartan, and I have a new red bow but it keeps coming loose.'

'So I see.' Aunt Jemima smiled. 'Tell me about your school, Meggie.'

Frustration turned Julia's eyes to a deep frown. She gazed helplessly at her errant offspring and strove to hide her anxiety. Meggie was 'way out of line, but short of making a scene and spoiling her aunt's pleasure in the child's company, she would be forced to give in gracefully.

Imperturbably Joel drew out another

chair. He threw her a mocking glance and spoke for her ears alone.

'Sit, Julia, and stop making like I'm a piranha. I don't bite.'

'All men bite!' Julia flared. 'Living with you lot is like juggling a bunch of hand grenades with the pins coming loose.'

'A jaundiced view, surely? It's obvious to me that the man you married must have been a complete jerk.'

The last statement was true enough, but none of it was his business.

'I haven't come here to debate my views with you, Doctor Mortimer. If you don't like them, tough.'

He grinned.

'In that case, we'll talk about your abominable weather instead. And since we are to be stuck with one another for the entire afternoon, please call me Joel. It's particularly off-putting to be toadied to at wedding receptions by beautiful women.'

Julia gave an outraged gasp.

'I never toady to anyone!'

'Then use my first name.'

She swallowed what felt like a lump of uncooked potato in her throat, and said his name just to show that it didn't matter a hoot. Joel leaned closer until one large shoulder touched hers, the fine material of his suit like a caress on her silk-clad arm.

'Another thing. Try not to look so sour. It's your sister's big day.'

'I'm well aware of that,' she snapped before taking a deep, steadying breath. 'Believe me, I am not sour. I couldn't be more happy for her.'

She took a sip of champagne and looked him directly in the eye.

'I apologise for my daughter's behaviour. You must find it embarrassing. Please take no notice. She's going through an awkward phase.'

A warmth crept into his steely eyes.

'Meggie? She's a delightful child. Seems perfectly normal to me.'

'She's a little unsettled at present, but I'm working on it.'

Casually, Joel placed an arm along

53

the back of her chair.

'Julia, single parenthood is no effortless task. There is exhaustion and frustration on a daily basis, not to mention a great deal of loneliness. From what I can see, you're doing a great job under difficult circumstances.'

At her look of amazement, he laughed. It was a rich, deep sound which did things to her insides. The charcoal eyes turned silver and the crinkles around them deepened attractively. Julia felt as though she had been dropped from a great height into a mass of warm honey. Her breath caught and she didn't quite know whether to like it or not. One thing she did know, this was not the reaction she should be having!

Joel topped up her champagne and handed her the glass. As though in a daze, Julia watched his strong, well-kept hands with their long, bronzed fingers and wondered how an academic could look like a man who spent his life out of doors. Surely historians sat huddled in dusty, old libraries with their noses in musty, old files. Come to think of it, with all that money, he probably had no need to work at all. He probably spent half his time in the Bahamas and the other half in the South of France, with all the women in creation after him.

Joel's fingers brushed hers as she took her glass. Julia flinched visibly. Worse, she found that she was actually trembling. She shouldn't be surprised at her reaction, she thought despairingly as the shock waves continued up her arm. Joel Mortimer's vibrant attraction was enough to excite any woman. There appeared to be another side of him, too, humour intelligence and compassion, a heady mixture, all that Carl had not been.

At the memory of her late husband, Julia's good sense returned. There was no way she was going down that road again! She would resist Dr Mortimer's attractions with every ounce of willpower it took.

It was dark when they emerged from

the hall at the end of the afternoon, Ginny and Tim having departed amidst many cheers in a suitably decorated vehicle with ribbons, tin cans and **Just Married** written on the back window. Another light drizzle had started, and tired little Meggie had run out of fuel.

'I don't want to go home, Mummy,' she wailed. 'I want to stay here, at the wedding.'

'The wedding is over, Meggie, and everyone is leaving. Aunt Jemima is coming to stay with us and we need to hurry home.'

Julia took Meggie by the hand, intent on walking her as fast as possible to their cottage in the lane. A large hand gripped her elbow.

'In you get, Julia. You'll come with us in the car,' Joel said firmly.

'No.'

Julia had spent an entire afternoon in his disturbing presence and couldn't get away fast enough.

'Thank you, but we prefer to walk.'

Joel uttered something under his

breath which sounded something like, 'Stubborn woman,' and tightened his grip.

'Don't be ridiculous. It's raining and you have no coat, and Meggie shouldn't be getting wet.'

He was right. Meggie already had a cough. It was foolish to insist on walking when they could ride. With a sigh she allowed herself to be shepherded into the luxurious depths of the car, suppressing the traitorous thought that it was pleasant to be cosseted for once.

The rain was falling in earnest by the time they stopped outside Julia's front door. She dashed up the steps to open the cottage as Joel assisted Aunt Jemima and Meggie into the house which was icier than Julia had anticipated. Dismayed, she went to switch on the heating. It was usually turned off in the afternoons in order to save money, but that hadn't been such a good idea today, had it?

Joel glanced around the small,

spotless living-room with its grey carpet and worn pink sofa. A vase of carnations stood on the mantelshelf. Julia had made the room cosy with cushions and a pink table lamp and matching velvet curtains drawn tightly against the cold. In two minutes he had the fire going, having deposited Aunt Jemima's suitcase in her room and settled her in an armchair while Julia went to make a cup of tea.

She instructed Meggie to get ready for bed and busied herself with the tray, peering into the small refrigerator while she waited for the kettle to boil. The farmer's wife had given her a dozen eggs yesterday, and she would add the last of her precious supply of cheese to the omelettes. It would have to be tinned peaches for dessert, if she could find any. It was frustrating, this business of constantly having to cut corners in order to make ends meet. Aunt Jemima was used to a good table, too. On Monday, she would have to steal a little of next week's rent money and go to the shops.

She carried the tray into the living-room and set it on the sofa table. Joel was standing before the fire, deep in conversation with Aunt Jemima. His voice was a deep, reassuring rumble which ceased abruptly the moment she entered. He shot her an enigmatic glance from veiled grey eyes and immediately declared himself ready to depart.

'You're going? But . . . '

Julia was suddenly and inexplicably overwhelmed by a feeling of near-panic. It was absurd. She felt as though her world was about to cave in.

'Tea?' she babbled. 'You'll not stay for some tea?'

The emotion had taken her completely by surprise. She must be more stressed out than she realised. The man was a mere acquaintance, and one she didn't even like. Why, then, all these useless, frustrating emotions? All right, so he looked like someone out of a movie, but so what? There were plenty of drop-dead-gorgeous hunks in the world. Why, then, did this particular man make her feel like the herd was getting ready to stampede?

Joel was observing her intently. She'd gone suddenly pale, and he wondered why. He declined the tea, kissed his godmother's cheek and surprised them all by announcing that he would be there in time to drive them to church in the morning.

'Then we're all going out to lunch,' he informed them firmly. 'There's a nice little place on the river.'

It would be a wonderful help not to have to find a midday meal for them all tomorrow. She found to her amazement that she'd like nothing better than to be taken out, and not by any man, by this man. She stared at Joel with wide, confused eyes. What was happening to her? She was a woman with a woman's needs but that didn't mean she had to turn into mush just because an attractive man appeared on the scene and showed them a bit of consideration.

She'd been on her own for five years now and she'd managed just fine. It had taken years to rebuild her self esteem after Carl, but she'd successfully put her life back on track. Life went on. It was no good nursing a wounded ego and refusing to be happy, because in some ways that was a greater crime than the one which had caused the state of affairs in the first place. Now, thankfully, she was a fairly self-contained young woman. She was secure in her own world and there was absolutely no room in that world for a man!

Joel was eyeing her in concern.

'Are you all right?'

'Perfectly,' Julia snapped, escorting him to the front door.

'Say good-night to Meggie for me.'

'Certainly.'

'I'll see you tomorrow then.'

Julia's mind was in a grey fog.

'Yes . . . no. I mean . . . look, I won't be . . .'

'Why don't we just get it over with?' Joel interrupted smoothly, placing his large hands on her shoulders.

'Get what over with?'

'This,' he replied and bent his head and took her mouth in a firm, possessive kiss.

At her gasp of surprise he smiled into her eyes, like a cat who had caught a mouse. Julia blinked once or twice while she readjusted her thinking.

She struggled for coherence, trying to ignore the deafening roar of blood in her ears and the clamour of her senses for more. She thrust him away, groping desperately for something to say. Seeing her predicament, Joe kissed her again.

'It's what we both wanted, isn't it?' he told her with a certain amount of masculine satisfaction. 'Good-night, Julia.'

He disappeared into the rain, leaving Julia too rattled to think. Joel's kisses had surprised her, to say the least.

Grinning to himself, Joel unlocked the car and climbed inside. The day hadn't gone too badly after all. He'd expected worse. Julia was a cool, little cat, but not quite as cool as she liked to pretend. Her response to his kisses had been interesting. But not as interesting as her probable reaction when she discovered exactly what he had in mind.

4

Julia tried to sleep, but failed miserably. For the first time in years her hard-won poise had deserted her. She was thoroughly unsettled, and it was all Joel Mortimer's fault! His kisses had reminded her of a fact she'd long since buried beneath layers of disillusion — she was still a woman, and a woman who needed to be loved.

She turned over and groaned. She would fight her growing attraction to Joel Mortimer. Somehow she would get through the next twenty-four hours with her emotions intact, and then her life could return to normal.

It was still raining in the morning which did nothing to lift the spirits. Joel had called their weather abominable, and she had to agree. As she stared out into the sodden garden Julia allowed her thoughts to wander into dangerous territory. What was it like in the sun of South Africa? Was there a woman in Joel's life? He must have gone to live there just after they'd met as youngsters, which was very likely the reason he'd never visited her parents' home again. She'd waited and waited, but he hadn't come back.

She tried to remember the snatches of family gossip she'd heard from Aunt Harriet, but all she could come up with was the fact that somehow or other, the Mortimer money was dirty. If she wanted to know any more she'd have to ask, and she had no intention of doing it. Aunt Harriet was frequently given to malicious exaggeration. She was one of those people who simply loved the smell of scandal.

Donning her black woollen skirt, black boots and pale blue sweater, Julia hurried to the kitchen to make Aunt Jemima's early-morning tea. The old lady always had her breakfast in bed, a simple meal of toast and marmalade.

Yesterday's post was still sitting on

the table in the tiny hallway. What with the wedding and Aunt Jemima's arrival, she hadn't had time to open it. She glanced at the bills and put them aside. There would be time enough on Monday to worry about them. There were one or two pieces of junk mail and a large white envelope with a London postmark. Curiously she slit open the top and removed a single sheet of paper.

As she read, Julia turned pale. It was from a firm of solicitors informing her that the cottage she was renting had been sold and the new owners wished to move in as soon as possible. They were hereby giving Mrs Julia Thornton one month's notice.

Julia gave a small cry. How could this be possible? Nothing had ever been said about selling, and she'd assumed she could stay as long as she liked. After all, they'd been here for nearly five years. The rent was unbelievably cheap, too. How would she be able to find something similar? She'd been very fortunate to hear about the cottage through Aunt Jemima just before Meggie's birth when she'd been quite desperate, and she had taken it at once. It was inconceivable that they were now being evicted.

Julia left the letter on the hall table and returned to the kitchen in a daze. There was nothing else to rent in the village that she knew of, and if she couldn't find something in the area she'd have to give up her two part-time jobs, which didn't bear thinking about.

Her jobs may be mundane, but they supplied enough for her and Meggie to get by on. She worked from Tuesday to Thursday in old Dr Dixon's surgery when Meggie was at playgroup in the village hall, and on Fridays she cleaned for the eccentric Mrs Cheney in the large house on the hill. On Saturdays she did her own housework and laundry, and on Mondays she went to the shops, which left only the evenings, once Meggie was in bed, for the great love of her life, her secret passion, writing.

Julia had not told anyone except Aunt Jemima about her children's books. She'd already published four and was busy working on the fifth, but it was too early to expect to be able to live off the proceeds. She'd taken other jobs to tide them over, but she longed to be free to write full-time.

Carl, who had simply disappeared from their lives, had never once offered to support his daughter and she wasn't prepared to take his money even if he had. It was best that both she and Meggie had nothing further to do with him. They were getting on with their lives.

Meggie padded into the kitchen, demanding her breakfast. She climbed on to a chair, picked up her spoon and tackled the porridge.

'Eat up, and then we'll take Aunt Jemima's breakfast tray upstairs.'

Meggie looked surprised. She'd forgotten that they had a house guest.

'Did my daddy sleep here, too?' she enquired hopefully.

Julia sighed.

'Dr Mortimer is not your father, Meggie, and, no, he did not sleep here.'

Meggie's mouth quivered.

'I want Dr Mortimer to sleep here! I want him to be my daddy. He said . . .'

'He said what?'

Meggie gave a watery smile which almost broke Julia's heart.

'He said he'd be honoured to be my daddy.'

'When exactly did he tell you this?' Julia demanded angrily.

How dare that insufferable man lead an impressionable child on in this fashion? Wait until she saw him!

'He said it at the wedding,' Meggie explained, 'when he helped me throw my roses and I asked him to be my daddy.'

Julia took a deep breath. They still had lunch to endure with him. The day was turning into a rotten one.

Meggie helped her clear the table

before they mounted the stairs with Aunt Jemima's breakfast tray. The old lady was sitting up in bed, reading from her little blue book of daily devotions. She peered at Julia over the top of her spectacles.

'You look a little tired and harassed today, my dear.'

Julia's lips tightened. It was all that man's fault! He'd filled every hour of her dreams with those enigmatic silver eyes, that attractive smile, those firm, exciting lips. She sent Meggie off to tidy her bedroom and perched on the end of Aunt Jemima's bed.

'Frankly, I'm fed up,' she confided. 'I don't know what I'm going to do.'

'Oh?'

Aunt Jemima listened to her news but did not seem unduly surprised.

'Joel did mention something about selling the cottage,' she said.

Julia's head snapped up.

'I beg your pardon?'

'Joel,' her aunt repeated. 'He told me he wanted to sell the cottage.'

'You mean Joel owns this cottage? Why didn't you say so before?'

'I thought you knew. It was he who suggested I contact you about it in the first place.'

'When was this?'

'Just before he returned to South Africa after studying for his doctorate. Carl had left, you were pregnant and you so desperately needed a place to stay. He bought the cottage especially so that you could rent it.'

'Is that why the rent is so cheap?' Julia demanded furiously. 'So he could play the great, caring benefactor? I won't take charity from anyone, Aunt, least of all a man like that. I'm perfectly able to pay my own way. I have always provided for my own daughter and shall continue to do so!'

Concern appeared in Aunt Jemima's eyes.

'Of course you have, dear, and a very good job you've made of it, too. You're a good mother, Julia, but then you had plenty of practice with your sisters, didn't you? I understand how you feel about Joel's generosity, but don't you think you're carrying your independence a little too far?'

'No, I am not! A woman can't be too independent as far as I'm concerned. I won't have any further interference from that hateful, smug, impossible man.'

To Julia's horror her voice cracked. Aunt Jemima drained her teacup.

'I shouldn't take it to heart, Julia. Something is bound to turn up. It always does,' she said calmly.

'How can you sit there and say that?'

'If I were you, I'd discuss it with Joel. He always knows what to do.'

Julia suppressed an angry snort. He was the last person to whom she'd turn now! She couldn't wait to see the last of him. It was as well he was nowhere in the vicinity at that precise moment, or she'd be tempted to commit some desperate, dark and dirty deed.

Unaware of her fierce opinion of him, Joel Mortimer was at that moment undertaking his own dirty work. He was sitting in his car, using his mobile phone in order to contact one or two old friends on the other side of Edinburgh.

'Robert? This is Joel. I want to thank you for finding a buyer for that cottage at such short notice. It will aid my plans considerably.'

He consulted his diary and dialled another number.

'Is that the Ace Detective Agency? Mr Charles Johnston, please.'

He tapped his fingers impatiently on the steering wheel as he waited.

'Charlie? Joel. Have you located Carl Thornton yet?'

He listened for a few minutes, grunted in satisfaction and wrote a few notes in his diary. Thornton was more of a scoundrel than he'd realised. The man ought to be behind bars. He sat staring at the information in his hand, pondering his best course of action. Coming to a firm decision, he held up his phone and punched in a number for

Johannesburg, South Africa.

'Thornton? My name is Mortimer. I have something to say to you.'

Well pleased with his morning's work, he switched on the ignition and drove to the cottage in time to escort the ladies to church where Julia, sitting beside him and conscious of him in such close proximity, heard not one word of the sermon. They emerged from the church to find that the rain had eased somewhat, with a watery sun trying its best to peer through a low bank of cloud. Joel drove them back to the cottage where he suggested a quiet drink before they left for the small inn where he'd reserved a table.

'Any glasses around, Julia?' he enquired hopefully, producing a bottle of Aunt Jemima's favourite sherry.

Julia, feeling as though she had lost the place completely, went into the kitchen to find them. Her earlier anger had left her with a fine colour which had deepened in an infuriating manner the moment she'd laid eyes on him.

'She's ready to spit,' Joel observed quietly, once she was out of earshot.

Aunt Jemima gave him a stern look.

'Yes. This cottage business has been a shock. Are you sure you know what you're doing, my boy?'

'Trust me, Aunt,' he replied with certainty.

Aunt Jemima gave a soft sigh.

'Oh, I do, I do, but Julia doesn't. She imagines that all men are like that ex-husband of hers. She's been through a lot, Joel. You must be patient.'

'I've wasted enough time already. It's time for action, serious action.'

Aunt Jemima chuckled.

'Well, you know what they say, dear. Desperate situations require desperate measures.'

They exchanged a look of mutual understanding.

'My thoughts exactly,' her godson agreed.

The inn was pleasantly full, with Sunday diners chatting over their roast beef and Yorkshire pudding. Pleasant music played in the background, a fitting accompaniment to the gracious room with its oak beams and inglenook fireplace. Julia had been there once before with Carl and despite the ambience of the room, the memory brought a knot to her stomach.

Joel seated Aunt Jemima first, and then Meggie. He pulled out Julia's chair and when she didn't respond, urged her with a large hand on the small of her back.

'Julia?'

Julia started guiltily. She'd been lost in her thoughts, most of them unpleasant. At Joel's touch, a warm shiver went through her, and she frowned. He had no right to affect her this way! She was unsettled enough as it was, and she still had to endure his disturbing presence all afternoon, not to mention those unreadable glances which seemed to tell her that he knew something which she didn't.

Meggie tucked into her meal with relish.

'I like this place,' she informed Joel happily. 'I like the food and I like the waitress with the pretty hair and I like the ducks and swans on the river. Can we come here again?'

'It's a date,' Joel assured her easily. 'What about next Sunday? I'll be staying in Edinburgh, but I'll drive up and fetch you.'

He stared at Julia, daring her to object. Finally he added in what she considered to be a particularly off-handed fashion, 'You had better come along, too, Mrs Thornton.'

'So kind,' she murmured sarcastically.

The silver-flecked eyes held a gleam of amusement.

'My pleasure.'

Children could be particularly infuriating sometimes, Julia reflected, hiding her chagrin behind her wine glass as she savoured another sip. Surprisingly, she found herself relaxing. The lamb chops and vegetables were excellent, as was the rather expensive wine Joel had chosen to accompany them. Even she could tell it was something special. The apple tart and cream, normally a rather mundane dessert, was total bliss. Meggie, quite unabashed, requested a third helping.

'Where do you put it all?' Joel enquired with a twinkle.

'In my tummy,' she replied logically. 'Mummy makes good apple tart but her porridge can be awful.'

Julia gave a rueful smile.

'It's not that bad but I did mess it up this morning. I had other things on my mind.'

Things like, where was she going to find a place to live? It was an excruciating embarrassment that he'd been her landlord all this time without her knowledge. Did he get his kicks out of giving anonymous hand-outs to poor little divorcees? And why? They meant nothing to each other.

Joel, watching her face, gave an inward sigh. When Julia looked up she surprised a look of compassion in his eyes, quickly masked, which only angered her further. She didn't need a man's pity!

'More coffee?' Joel offered smoothly.

'No, thank you. It was a lovely meal, thank you. If you're quite finished, Meggie, I think we should go.'

Dusk was falling when they finally reached the cottage, Joel having decided to drive Aunt Jemima around Perthshire before giving them afternoon tea in the garden of another small inn. There, Meggie seemed happier than usual, slipping her hand into Joel's with trusting familiarity as they strolled along the riverbank. It was unacceptable that he did nothing to discourage the child's regard. Once he'd disappeared from their lives Meggie would be asking for him, she had little doubt of that. And who would be left to pick up the pieces?

Joel now assisted Aunt Jemima into the house where the old lady declared herself unable to eat another thing. She would take herself up to her bedroom instead, if Julia didn't mind.

'Of course not, Aunt,' Julia agreed.

Once Aunt Jemima had disappeared, Joel kissed Meggie on the cheek and took the words out of Julia's mouth by instructing the child to go upstairs and have her bath. It was too much! The anger which had been mounting all day spilled over.

'I would appreciate it if you would mind your own business,' Julia told him furiously. 'You've been acting as though you own us, Meggie and me. Let me lay it bluntly on the line. I want you to stay out of our affairs.'

Joel leaned against the kitchen door, his face inscrutable.

'Is that what you think? That I would like to own you?'

'Yes, and I won't be owned! You're one of the most high-handed, interfering, self-satisfied men I've ever met. You've been pulling our strings for years, haven't you?'

He gave her a long, enigmatic stare.

'Do you mind telling me exactly what

it is I am supposed to have done?'

'With pleasure. You bought this cottage just so we could live in it. You failed to charge me the full rental. You've upped and sold it from under our feet when it suits you. You've appeared out of nowhere and disrupted our lives. Now you've stolen Meggie's heart.'

Her voice rose alarmingly and the treacherous sheen of moisture filmed her eyes. She blinked, determined not to cry in front of him.

'I won't say you haven't meant to be kind, but I want to make it clear that I won't stand for it any longer.'

Joel's gaze never left her face. He straightened up, almost having to duck his head as he stepped through the doorway into the tiny kitchen.

'We need to talk.'

'Talk?' Julia said shrilly. 'What is there to talk about? I won't listen to any further manipulation! I've had my say and I would appreciate it if you would now leave my home.'

She controlled her quivering mouth long enough to go on thoughtlessly.

'And take your bedroom eyes with you because I don't need any further complications in my life. I don't need . . . don't need . . . '

She trailed off, appalled at what she'd just implied.

'A man?' Joel supplied blandly. 'Are you telling me you're frigid, Julia?'

'Certainly not! Not that it's any of your business.'

Wrong, Joel thought, shoving his hands into his pockets to keep them from reaching for her. His next words stunned her.

'Julia, I want you to come to Africa with me.'

Her mouth dropped open in a rather unbecoming gape. Then she shook her head in angry disgust.

'You're crazy, do you know that?'

'Not crazy. Just . . . '

'Trying to take charge again? You think you know what's best for me and Meggie, right?'

'No. I'm just doing what I know to be the right thing.'

Julia had had enough. It had been a very stressful day. Heck, it had been a very stressful week, so much so that it was beginning to feel as though she were diagonally parked in a parallel universe!

She poked a slim, pink-tipped finger at his chest.

'We have nothing whatsoever to talk about, least of all Africa. I'd like you to leave. Now!'

Furiously she bundled him out of the front door and only then remembered her manners, adding with cold finality, 'Thank you for buying us lunch, Doctor Mortimer. Please understand there will be no dining out next Sunday for Meggie and me.'

Once Meggie was in bed Julia hauled out the vacuum cleaner, needing to do something physical in order to dispel her frustration. She'd been rude, but Joel Mortimer couldn't say he hadn't had it coming to him. She'd never met a man she disliked more. Africa indeed! The very thought was preposterous.

Her nerves had been taut for days. Aunt Jemima was right, she needed to chill out for a bit, but not until she'd cleaned the house!

Later, Julia lay in the bath for a long time in order to reflect upon her day. She could make no sense out of it at all, and her unhappy thoughts only served to dampen her spirits further so that she felt a great, hot tear scald her cheek. The water had grown cold and she climbed out, berating herself for being a self-pitying idiot. But the truth was, there was only so much a girl could take. Shivering, she dried herself, pulled on her nightgown and climbed into a very cold bed. It was an unpleasant end to what should have been a most pleasant weekend.

★　★　★

Joel Mortimer paced the carpet and dragged a hand through his well-styled hair. A heavy frown settled on his brow. He'd never met a more desirable woman in his life and he ached with wanting her, so much so that he'd allowed his feelings to overrule his better judgement. He shouldn't have blurted out his plan like that. He should have taken it more slowly, waited until Julia was ready. The result had been counter-productive. Aunt Jemima was right. Julia was a woman who would not be rushed.

If he hadn't known her history he'd say she was the most uptight female he'd ever met, one with a talent for finding difficulties where none existed. After all, what could be more easy than up and relocating to another country at the drop of a hat? His lips curved into a self-deprecating grin. To be honest, she'd taken it better than he'd expected. After all, he was only asking her to accompany him, a virtual stranger, into the wilds of South Africa at a moment's notice and for no logical reason, with a small child in tow. What had he imagined? That she'd fall over herself in anticipation?

He picked up his keys, locked the door and headed off for breakfast in the small village inn.

Joel glanced around the near-empty dining-room and thought longingly of Marta's cooking back home. Hopefully there would be an improvement on last night's fare because he had some serious thinking to do. He had to figure out his next move, and a man couldn't very well think on an empty stomach. He munched his way through an enormous plate of bacon, eggs, sausages, mushrooms and toast, lost in the logistics of transporting his future wife and her beguiling four-year-old daughter back to South Africa.

* * *

Meggie awoke before it was quite light and crept into Julia's bed. The child's cough had deteriorated during the night, leaving her feverish.

'Chest hurts, Mummy,' she sobbed.

Julia roused herself from a particularly unpleasant dream where she was being dragged off to Africa against her wish, leaving Meggie on Joel's shoulder as they threw confetti all over Aunt Jemima.

'Chest is sore. Throat, too,' Meggie repeated.

Julia sat up and felt her forehead.

'Poor love, you're burning. We'll have to visit Dr Dixon again, won't we?'

'Don't want to,' Meggie mumbled, and fell into an uneasy sleep.

Julia sighed. She might as well get up and start the chores while Meggie was asleep because there would be no opportunity later. Meggie would need constant attention, and everything else would have to be shelved. Just as soon as the surgery opened she'd take Meggie along, but Dr Dixon wouldn't exactly be pleased to see them. This was Meggie's third bout of bronchitis and it wasn't even mid-winter yet.

After breakfast Julia bundled Meggie

into her padded coat and left Aunt Jemima in the living-room in front of the fire, complete with a pile of books and Saturday's crossword puzzle. With a promise to be as quick as she could, she informed her aunt that a tea tray was ready and waiting in the kitchen should she require it.

'Don't you worry about me, my dear. Just get Meggie sorted out,' Aunt Jemima urged.

For once it wasn't raining but the wind was cold, chilling them to the bone. Meggie coughed the whole way to the surgery. Although it was Julia's day off, she arrived early enough to help Cilla McGuire, the other receptionist, tidy the waiting-room before the patients arrived. Fortunately, she and Meggie would be first in the queue.

The elderly doctor, having been in country practice for many years, was well used to fretful small children. He coaxed Meggie out of her misery just long enough to examine her thoroughly before surveying Julia.

'I'd like her lungs X-rayed,' he said. 'Take her along to the cottage hospital tomorrow morning, and in the meantime we'll put her on a stronger antibiotic. Don't bother to come in for work tomorrow. Cilla can manage.'

Julia thanked him, hiding her dismay.

'The sore chest, it's not pneumonia, is it?'

'No, my dear, but we shall have to be careful. A few days' warmth and cosseting won't come amiss, with plenty of fluids. And keep her quiet.'

He removed his spectacles, leaned back in his chair and observed them thoughtfully.

'You look as though you could do with a break, yourself, Julia. When did you last take a holiday?'

What's a holiday, she thought ruefully. Aloud she said, 'Not for ages, Doctor.'

'I would advise you to get away to a warmer place for a while. This climate doesn't appear to suit Meggie.'

He took a moment to consult the file in front of him.

'I shouldn't like her to be debilitated any further this winter by another bout of bronchitis. Give a possible holiday some thought if you can.'

Julia thanked him and ushered Meggie from the room, her spirits lower. It was all very well speaking of holidays, but where on earth was she to get the money to afford one? Julia ensured that Meggie's hat, scarf and gloves were snugly in place before braving the wind once more. They collected Meggie's prescribed medicine from the chemist and stopped at the corner shop to buy a packet of sausages. There would be no time for a full grocery shop. It would have to be sausage and mash this evening.

Before leaving the warmth of the shop Julia paused to examine the contents of her purse. There was just enough money left for a pint of milk. She would make Meggie an egg custard for her lunch.

As they turned into the lane Julia's heart set up a furious pounding. Parked outside her home was the familiar Mercedes, and standing beside it, about to lock its door, was Joel Mortimer.

5

Joel turned at the sound of their approach and greeted them politely, his gaze narrowed on Meggie's white face.

'What have you done with her? She looks ill.'

It was a remark not calculated to put Julia in the best of tempers. How dare he imply that she was a negligent mother!

'She is ill,' Julia told him sweetly, 'and if any blame is to be attached, I'd say it's all your fault. I wasn't the one who dragged us out along icy riverbanks yesterday afternoon.'

It was hardly a fair accusation and she immediately felt ashamed. The truth was, he'd put himself out to give them all a pleasant outing.

'I'm sorry, I shouldn't have said that. It's just that you infuriate me.'

'So I've noticed.'

He didn't sound in the least put out.

'What do you want?' she demanded, hoping he would state his business and go.

Those bedroom eyes would be her undoing yet, she just knew it.

'Such warm hospitality,' he mocked, pocketing his keys. 'I've come to see my godmother.'

'Oh.'

Julia knew she'd been rude again, but he had the unfortunate knack of bringing out the worst in her.

'You'd better come in, then.'

Turning abruptly, she bundled Meggie into the house. Joel followed, his frustration well hidden. The woman was as prickly as a cushion full of pins. He'd have to play it cool, or risk jeopardising the whole plan.

'Well?' Aunt Jemima asked as soon as she saw them.

'Meggie's going to be fine,' Julia told her quickly.

She smiled brightly to reassure everyone and began to remove Meggie's coat.

'We'll just pop you into bed, Meggie, and then I'll make something nice for your lunch.'

Once they were out of earshot, Joe turned to Aunt Jemima.

'Problems?'

'So it seems. Meggie isn't a particularly robust child.'

'Anything I can do? Do they eat properly? Does Julia need any money?' Aunt Jemima rolled her eyes heavenwards.

'Don't even think about it! She'd chew you up and spit you out.'

'What makes you think she hasn't done so already?'

The old lady chuckled.

'Have patience, dear. The end result will be worth waiting for.'

'That's what I keep telling myself.'

Julia reappeared on her way to the kitchen, clutching Meggie's hot water bottle.

'Tea?' she offered in a businesslike voice.

Aunt Jemima brightened.

'That would be lovely, but tell me first, what exactly did the doctor say?'

Julia's eyes grew shadowed.

'It appears that Meggie has a weak chest. He wants an X-ray taken tomorrow morning at ten, and he's given us stronger medication.'

'It's my opinion that this climate is wrong for her,' Aunt Jemima stated. 'Meggie needs somewhere hot and dry.'

Julia nodded unhappily.

'That's exactly what Dr Dixon said.'

Joel, sensing his opportunity, jumped in with both feet.

'Why not reconsider my suggestion, Julia? Come to South Africa with me. Consider it a holiday, with all the expenses paid.'

Julia went scarlet.

'Thank you, but no, thank you. Don't you think you've done enough already?'

She clutched at the hot water bottle, her knuckles showing white.

'Frankly, no. I'd like to be able to do more, if you'll let me. I don't see what the big deal is.'

Julia rounded on him furiously.

'Then allow me to enlighten you! It's called self-respect, and I have plenty of it. Can you understand that?'

She stormed off to the kitchen and gave vent to her feelings by slamming a few cupboards.

'Oh, dear,' Aunt Jemima murmured.

Joel suppressed a grin.

'I shall forego the tea, I think. Tell Julia I'll be here in time to take them to the hospital tomorrow. Meggie must not walk about in this weather.'

'I agree with you.'

'I'll run you back to little Crawford in the afternoon, if that's all right with you. I have to be in Edinburgh for a dinner engagement in the evening.'

He bent and kissed his godmother's cheek.

'Don't look so dismayed. I'm not finished by a long shot. I'll let Julia think she's won this round. It'll sweeten her up for the next. Make no mistake, I'll win in the end.'

'And you always play to win, don't you, Joel?' Aunt Jemima twinkled. 'Particularly when Mortimer honour is at stake. If you can pull this off, your grandfather would be delighted, wherever he is.'

'Yes, but I'm not doing this for Seth. I'm not doing it for Mortimer honour, either. Just for the record, I'm not even doing it for myself.'

He paused at the door.

'I'm doing it for Julia,' he said clearly.

After lunch, Julia telephoned the local estate agent for advice on properties to rent. She was regretfully informed that there was nothing available in the village, and very little else beyond. Trying not to feel too disheartened, she thanked the woman and rang off. The second agent had much the same advice, as did the third. The only properties they had were too far away, completely unsuitable or simply outside

Julia's price range. Despairingly, she replaced the receiver.

'Any luck?' Aunt Jemima enquired.

'No. I just don't know what I'm going to do.'

Aunt Jemima considered for a moment.

'I may be able to help. I can offer to have you and Meggie for one month, which will give you a little more time to find something.'

Julia shook her head.

'I couldn't put you out. Anyway, Little Crawford is thirty minutes away. What about my jobs?'

'Find others,' Aunt Jemima declared robustly.

'It's not as easy as that. That could take months,' Julia enlightened her.

Meggie coughed all that night and awoke in the morning as fretful as ever. She refused breakfast and declared she was not going to the hospital, and nobody was taking a picture of her chest.

'Jamie had a picture taken at the

hospital and Jamie said there's an ugly doctor there who looks like one of the seven dwarves,' she stated. 'Jamie says he hurts little children.'

'That's just nonsense,' Julia told her firmly.

She managed to coax Meggie into taking a little scrambled egg but when it was time to get dressed, Meggie hid under the bedcovers.

'Meggie!'

Meggie poked her nose out from under the duvet.

'Yes, Mummy?'

Julia said firmly, 'You are going to have that X-ray today whether you like it or not. So you might as well get up. Now!'

'Don't want to,' Meggie wailed, ducking under the covers again.

Julia spent the next few minutes pleading and threatening, all to no avail. Hearing a sound in the doorway which sounded suspiciously like a laugh, she spun around.

'Trouble?' Joel enquired blandly.

'Nothing I can't handle,' Julia flung at him crossly.

How long had he been standing there? She hoped he hadn't witnessed Meggie's tantrum because it reflected badly on her ability to discipline the child, and that made her look like an incompetent mother. Joel put his hand under the duvet and grabbed Meggie by the foot.

'Come out, fair maid, or I'll have your toes for sausages.'

Meggie stopped in mid-wail. Her head appeared above the covers and she gave a delighted giggle.

'Are you hungry, Mister Wolf? Mummy will make you scrambled eggs.'

Joel yanked off the offending duvet.

'I've already eaten. Get dressed, Meggie,' he instructed in a no-nonsense voice, 'or we'll be late for your appointment.'

To Julia's amazement, Meggie obeyed. She even took her medication without fuss. Then with her coat and hat snugly in place, she slipped her hand into Joel's.

'Let's go,' she urged him between coughs. 'I'm not afraid of dwarves.'

Julia was silent as they drove to the hospital. The previous half hour had been an eye-opener. It had told her one thing loud and clear — Meggie very definitely needed a father.

Despairingly, she gazed at the winter fields and frozen ponds. What was she to do now? She looked into the future and saw only years of relentless, unshared responsibility, as if she hadn't already endured them, raising her two sisters! Quite honestly, the very thought of such a future filled her with dread. She'd had to assume too much responsibility too quickly, and she'd burned herself out. All she wanted now was for someone else to take charge. But to give Meggie a father meant finding a husband, something she had absolutely no intention of doing. So it was back to square one.

It was at that point that Julia decided

to sell her mother's rings. As soon as Meggie was better she would find the time to go to the pawnbroker in the village. It was time to part with the treasured keepsakes, and she knew her mother would be the first to agree. Meggie would have that holiday, come what may! A package deal in Greece or Spain, perhaps? Julia leaned back against the cream leather and relaxed.

Meggie behaved perfectly throughout the appointment, darting Joel loving glances in between bouts of coughing. He complimented her afterwards as they climbed into the car, stating that her reward would be a visit to the fish and chip shop on the way home. At this news, Meggie's pale little face lit up. After a happy family meal taken informally in the kitchen, she went back to bed and was as good as gold for the rest of the day.

Aunt Jemima hugged Julia and declared herself quite ready to depart.

'Thank you for a lovely visit, Julia,

and don't forget that my door is always open.'

Joel took his godmother's suitcase to the car and returned to assist her down the steps.

'I won't say goodbye, Julia. We're bound to meet again before I return to South Africa,' he said casually.

'I doubt it,' she replied, remaining in the doorway to wave them off.

She had never felt more lonely in her entire life.

Julia managed to persuade her neighbour, Mrs Heslop, to sit with Meggie for the next two days while she went to the surgery, offering to do her week's laundry in exchange. The days flew by, and heavy frosts began to blanket the countryside. Soon Christmas decorations appeared in the village shops, their brightness bringing a cheer Julia tried hard to embrace.

Ginny and Tim arrived back from their honeymoon looking tanned and happy, already making plans for Christmas, when Kirsty and her new husband were to be arriving from Glasgow to stay. The twins appeared to be so taken up with their own lives, they barely gave Julia a thought, which only added to her increasing sense of loneliness.

On the Friday evening Julia sat down to write out her Christmas cards. Meggie was in bed and the ironing had all been neatly folded away. What with Meggie's illness, looking for alternative accommodation and being rushed off her feet at work, there had been no time as yet to plan their holiday, so her mother's rings were still sitting upstairs in the jewellery box. Her priority was to find her and Meggie somewhere to stay.

Unfortunately Meggie's cough had not improved as much as she'd hoped. The child still looked pale. After Christmas she would set things in motion for that trip abroad.

Mechanically, she signed her name on a few of the cards, wishing she could go to bed. The practice nurse had been off with flu and they'd been kept on the run at the surgery all week with the usual seasonal ailments. She was tired, her feet ached and she was in no mood for visitors, so at the strident ringing of the doorbell, Julia froze. She crept cautiously to the front door and peered through the peephole. She'd never quite been able to conquer a certain nervousness on hearing the doorbell at night.

Two people stood on the front steps, sharing a large umbrella which shielded their faces from her view. A couple of salesmen, she thought, or people peddling catalogues. Julia flung open the door hoping to make short work of the unwelcome pair but before she could speak she was thrust aside as they barged roughly into the hall.

'Excuse me!' she gasped.

'Sorry, darling,' Carl Thornton drawled, removing the scarf which covered the lower half of his face. 'I thought you might refuse us entry, so I wasn't taking any chances.'

Shocked to the core, Julia could only

gaze dumbly into his podgy face. The years had not been kind, she thought, but then, he'd always had the tendency to run to fat. What had she ever seen in him?

He smiled nastily.

'Cat got your tongue, Julia? You always used to have plenty to say.'

Insultingly, his cold eyes roved her body.

'Can't say you've improved much, either. Still the same flat chest.'

His goading had its effect. Julia flushed hotly. Her body may be slim, but she knew perfectly well it was shapely, despite Carl's deliberate put-down.

'Get out of my house or I'll call the police.'

Carl laughed derisively.

'Not so fast. We've come a long way, Julia, and you'll listen to what we have to say. We're not leaving until you do.'

Julia scrutinised the woman by his side. She was a tall redhead, taller than

Carl and particularly voluptuous. Her green eyes were slits in her heavily-made-up face and they darted assessingly around Julia's small home, obviously finding it inadequate.

'Not much of a place to bring up a child, is it?' she asked maliciously.

Julia controlled her outrage.

'Just who is this woman?' she demanded.

Carl looked smug.

'My wife, Leandra. Isn't she gorgeous?'

Leandra Thornton tossed him a disdainful glance and said in a bored voice, 'Say what you have to say, Carl. We haven't all that much time. The hotel stops serving dinner at nine.'

Carl was obviously trying to decide his best option. He immediately turned on the charm.

'Julia, darling, may we sit down? A cup of coffee wouldn't come amiss. That's one thing Leandra can't do, make good coffee, at least, not like yours, my dear Julia.'

Julia didn't bother to hide her disgust.

'I shall not be serving coffee. Like your wife says, say what you have to say, Carl.'

With a shrug Carl pushed past her into the living-room and flopped down on to the pink sofa, followed unwillingly by his companion.

'Seeing you're in one of your moods, Julia,' he sneered, 'I'll get to the point. I've come for the child.'

Julia's heart went into freefall. With an enormous effort she took a very firm grip on her emotions.

'What child?' she managed calmly.

Alarm crept into Carl's eyes.

'You had the brat, didn't you? You were pregnant when I left. I distinctly remember you refusing to get rid of it.'

'Too right,' Julia agreed sweetly. 'Why deny a child the right to live, just because its father is a jerk?'

Carl's face turned ugly.

'I have reason to believe you have a daughter.'

'So?'

'I'm here to see her.'

'Why?'

He hadn't bothered for four years, so why now?

Carl dropped his gaze, unable or unwilling to give any reasons.

'It doesn't matter why. I'm here. Where is she?'

'Staying with a friend,' Julia lied.

Who did Carl think he was? She wouldn't put it past him to go barging into Meggie's bedroom to waken her, a traumatic experience for any child. Oddly, something like relief crept into Carl's eyes.

'Well now, isn't that just too bad?'

Julia gazed pointedly at Leandra Thornton's empty left hand. The woman was no more married to him than she was Old Mother Hubbard! What was the odious pair up to? She didn't have long to wait.

'I'd like to make you an offer,' Carl stated firmly.

Julia kept her voice steady as she

asked, 'What kind of an offer?'

'Leandra here can't have children. She's pining for a child, aren't you, darling?'

A fierce glare in Leandra's direction forbade any disagreement. She nodded in sulky agreement.

'Actually, we want full custody. We'll pay you well,' he continued.

He named a sum, and Julia could hardly believe her ears.

'You're offering to buy her?'

'Why not? It'll save going to court.'

Rage roared through her like an express train.

'In my book you have no legal or parental rights whatsoever. You forfeited them when you walked out, Carl! There is absolutely no way I would ever give up my child, so you can take your stinking offer and leave. Now!'

Carl went red with anger.

'Not so hasty. You know me better than that, Julia. I'm a man who always gets what he wants.'

He stamped into the hall.

'I'll fight you in court. You haven't heard the last of this, my snooty little ex! I want the child, and so help me, I'll get the child.'

Shocked and furious, Julia slammed the door in his face. If she'd had problems before, it was nothing compared to this! Carl Thornton was right about one thing — he would use any means he could. He was quite capable of resorting to kidnap in order to get his own way, which meant that as from this moment, little Meggie was at risk.

She returned to the sitting-room and threw herself into a chair. The creep hadn't even once referred to his child by name. He probably didn't even know it! What kind of a monster was he? There was no way under heaven she'd give Meggie up, Julia determined fiercely. For the first time since the death of her parents, she dropped her head into her hands and wept.

Once she was calmer, she tried to think. No doubt Carl would begin to badger her, appearing at every turn, just like he had when he'd tried to get her to marry him. It wouldn't be long before Meggie demanded to know who he was, and being so desperate for a father, she'd probably agree to go with him. That awful woman, whoever she was, would become Meggie's stepmother. It didn't bear thinking about.

In the morning Julia dressed Meggie in warm clothes and put on a cheerful face.

'We're going into the village today, Meggie.'

'Why, Mummy? It's Saturday.'

'I know. We'll do the housework when we get back. I thought we'd have a little treat. How about tea and scones, and your favourite comic?'

Meggie brightened.

'All right, Mummy.'

Julia went upstairs and slipped the small box containing her mother's rings into her handbag. The pawnbroker's shop was right next door to the tearoom.

With a few days left until Christmas,

cheerful lights were hung all along the main street, brightening the dull morning. Conscious that Meggie's cough was still troubling her, Julia hurried her into the warmth of the tea shop where they spent a pleasant half hour. She paid the bill, took Meggie by the hand and left, only to find that the pawnbroker next door was closed. A notice was stuck in the window. Old Mr Grant, it appeared, had flu.

Suppressing her impatience, Julia hurried Meggie home. She'd have to find time on Monday to pawn those rings, the sooner, the better. With Carl now hanging around, a holiday seemed more than ever imperative. On no account must he set eyes on his vulnerable little daughter. If the worst came to the worst, she and Meggie would simply disappear.

It began to drizzle as they hurried up the garden path. Julia reached into her pocket for the door key, looked up to insert it and almost fainted.

'Hello, Julia,' Carl drawled from the

doorstep. 'Where the dickens have you been all morning? I've been waiting for you.'

He glanced incautiously at Meggie.

'That, I suppose, is your brat.'

Julia wanted to hit him. After her initial fright, she found her voice and it was surprisingly strong.

'What do you want?'

'I want to negotiate. I can't stand out here in the rain. Let's go inside.'

He barged in front of her. What had happened to those patently false manners he'd adopted when he was courting her, Julia wondered. Meggie followed with huge eyes.

'Who is that man, Mummy?'

Before she could reply Carl cut in nastily.

'I'm your father.'

Julia glared at him, dreading Meggie's reaction and hoping the child wouldn't be too traumatised by the sudden, unwelcome appearance of this awful, insensitive man. He was the last thing to a father she would ever desire for her child. Meggie regarded him blankly.

'No, you're not,' she stated. 'My daddy is Dr Mortimer. I like him better.'

And without further interest, she went upstairs with her new magazine. Julia almost laughed. Good for Meggie! Carl opened his mouth and closed it again before stabbing Julia with an ugly glance.

'That's because the little rat knows which side her bread's buttered. She's a chip off the old block. Yours! You always were a gold-digger, and I know this Mortimer. He obviously has plenty of gold.'

'That is untrue, and you know it,' Julia said coldly.

Whatever it was Carl wished to say, he had better say it quickly.

'Only a gold-digger would marry a man like Mortimer,' Carl insisted, 'which brings me to the business in hand. Tell Mortimer that I'll back off if he pays me ten grand. Not a penny less, see? He can adopt your brat for all I care. I'll give my consent, no problem. But if my demand is not met, I'll proceed with court action for custody. I'll give you until Monday. Tell him if he doesn't play ball, I'll fight you both, tooth and nail.'

6

To Julia's disgust it was still raining on Sunday morning. There was no question of taking Meggie to church in this weather so after breakfast she turned on the television for the televised service, from Edinburgh.

'God is able to make every situation work out for your good,' the minister was saying.

Julia stared at the screen. Did that include even the sudden intrusion into their lives of Carl Thornton with his unspeakable evil? And what about the disturbing Joel Mortimer, and Meggie's health, and their much-needed holiday, and having to find a new home? Despite her doubts she closed her eyes and offered up a small prayer for help.

On Monday morning before breakfast, the telephone rang. Julia, not quite awake after her restless night, snatched the receiver off the hook.

'Did you tell Mortimer I want that ten grand?' Carl demanded.

'I haven't seen him yet, Carl. I'll only be seeing him on Christmas day,' she hedged.

If she and Meggie could move out of the cottage by then, Carl wouldn't be able to find them. Carl swore vividly.

'Make sure that you do, Julia. I warn you, I am not playing games.'

Julia went into the kitchen to make herself a cup of tea. Where had Carl got the perverted idea that Joel wanted to adopt Meggie, or that she'd even be prepared to marry him? One minute Carl was offering to buy his own daughter and the next he was trying to extort money to be rid of her. Nothing made sense.

She tossed a teabag into a mug and covered it with boiling water. Once Carl discovered that she had no intention of involving Joel Mortimer in her affairs by informing him of these outrageous demands, she had little doubt that her odious ex-husband would try to snatch Meggie at the earliest opportunity and hold them all to ransom.

Julia ladled Meggie's porridge into a blue china bowl and shoved the pan back on the cooker with trembling fingers. There was so much which didn't quite add up, like, how did Carl know about Joel Mortimer in the first place? Were they in cahoots?

As soon as Meggie was occupied with tidying her bedroom, Julia decided it was time for action. She went to the telephone.

'May I take you up on that offer of a place to stay?' she asked Aunt Jemima, hoping that her voice sounded normal. 'We still haven't found other accommodation and we have to be out of the cottage by the end of December. I know it's a lot to ask, what with Christmas and everything.'

Aunt Jemima responded quickly.

'I'd be delighted, dear. When would you like to come?'

'As soon as I've packed up our

clothes. We don't have much, Aunt. Most of the furniture belongs to the cottage.'

'I'll have the room ready,' Aunt Jemima promised, hiding her surprise. 'There's some storage space in the attic, as well. You won't mind sharing a room with Meggie?'

'No, not at all. I'm very grateful to you.'

Julia rang off, anxious and relieved at the same time. There was no time to be lost. She'd begin sorting their clothes.

At the same time, Aunt Jemima replaced the receiver and frowned. It was strange that Julia wished to arrive so soon. Something had happened to make her sound so rattled. At the earliest opportunity she would inform Joel. He would know just what to do.

Joel had just returned to the hotel after giving his final lecture to a group of museum curators. He removed his jacket, dialled room service in preference to going down to the dining-room and switched on the television in time to hear the evening news. Not being particularly interested in the headlines, he turned off the sound and fell to thinking about Julia. Was she coping? Had Meggie's cough improved any? On impulse, he reached for his mobile phone.

Julia, up to her knees in piles of clothing, extricated herself and went to answer the phone with her heart in her mouth. Supposing it was Carl again?

'Yes?' she whispered, hoping the jangling hadn't awakened Meggie.

'Julia, it's Joel.'

His deep voice wrapped her in a warm blanket of reassurance and she gave a great sigh of relief.

'Oh, thank goodness. I thought . . . '

'You thought what?'

'I thought it was someone else.'

To her dismay Julia's voice wobbled, and there was a brief silence.

'Julia, is everything all right? Meggie isn't ill again?' Joel said then.

'No, Meggie's just fine. At least, she's not any worse.'

'But she's not much better, is that it?'

'Well, no, I suppose she isn't. I've had to send her back to her playgroup in the village hall, though. I have to go to work. It's only for a few hours a day. I'm doing the best I can.'

Annoyed that she felt the need to explain herself, her voice became tart.

'Anyway, we'll be taking a holiday soon, just as soon as we've finished staying with Aunt Jemima.'

There, that should show him that she had everything under control.

'I don't understand. You're moving in with your aunt? When?'

'Just as soon as I can pack up here.'

Joel frowned. She sounded frightened and desperate.

'Is there anything I can do to help? I'm up in Edinburgh tomorrow.'

'You are?' Julia gasped.

For no reason at all life suddenly seemed brighter.

'In that case, could you . . . would you . . . '

What was she saying? She was

actually begging his help, but this was no time to allow her stupid pride to stand in the way. Meggie's safety came first.

'How soon can you get here?' she asked.

With Joel on the scene, she and Meggie would both be far safer.

Thoughtfully, Joel rang off. After holding him at a distance for days, Julia was now prepared to rely on his assistance. Something was very definitely up, and he had every intention of finding out what it was. He cancelled the order for room service, flung some clothes into his suitcase and went downstairs to pay the bill. Within minutes the Mercedes was nosing its powerful way through the London traffic.

Next morning, the waitress at the Angler's Bait was amazed to see Joel at his table again, eating his way through a hearty breakfast. He must have arrived late because she hadn't seen him when she'd gone off duty at midnight the previous evening.

'Coffee, sir?' she enquired.

Joel looked up blankly.

'Oh . . . er, no, thank you.'

The coffee could wait. He intended to arrive at Julia's cottage just as soon as it was decent. With his thoughts on Meggie and the possibility of obtaining an appointment with a paediatrician just as soon as was possible, he left the dining-room.

Meggie was still in bed. At Joel's ring Julia peered around the door chain as though she'd been expecting a burglar. She gave a shaky smile.

'Good morning.'

Her previous air of angry defiance had been replaced by a touching vulnerability.

'Please, come in,' she invited formally.

Intrigued, Joel greeted her with a chaste kiss on the cheek.

'Why do I get the feeling,' he asked as he surveyed the living-room which was now empty of cushions, books and table lamps, 'that you're moving out in rather a hurry?'

'We are,' Julia replied, deciding to be honest.

He kept his voice casual.

'Any particular reason?'

'Something came up. I thought it was for the best.'

'Do you mind telling me what it was?'

She wanted so desperately to trust this man, but could she? She was saved from reply by the strident ringing of the doorbell. Turning pale, she shot a frightened look at Joel before going to answer it.

Carl's voice was belligerent as he pushed past her into the hall.

'I've decided that I'm not prepared to wait until Christmas, Julia. I want to contact Mortimer immediately, is that clear? I want that money.'

Even at this early hour, his breath smelt of liquor.

'Where is your wife?' Julia hedged, trying to distract him. 'Has she changed her mind about wanting a child?'

Carl blinked.

'Wife?'

It took a moment before he remembered.

'Oh, you mean Leandra? She left me and went back to Johannesburg. Did you ask Mortimer about the money?'

'No. I told you I won't see him until Christmas.'

Carl took a step towards her, looking livid.

'I won't wait,' he yelled, giving her a shove.

Joel, standing near the door, moved like lightning. He placed a protective arm about Julia's shoulders and enquired silkily, 'Who is this man, darling?'

Carl recovered from his surprise and gave a knowing grin.

'You must be Mortimer. I knew she was lying! I'm Thornton. Julia's ex.'

Joel's voice was deceptively mild.

'Well, Thornton, I'd ask you into the living-room but your manners in front of a lady appear to be sadly lacking. What is it exactly that you want?'

Carl took a step backward, obviously intimidated by Joel's size.

'You will remember that you telephoned me in South Africa. Well, I took the first flight out and I'm here to make you an offer.'

Joel's jaw hardened.

'I see. And what is this offer?'

'I'll drop all court action to get custody of the child if you will pay me ten thousand pounds, pronto. I repeat, immediately.'

'Indeed?' Joel said coldly.

'Well? Do you accept my offer or not?'

Joel pretended to consider.

'Oh, I think not. I know all about your little insurance scams and how you rob little old ladies and persist in keeping all those investors in the dark.'

'I d-don't know what you mean,' Carl stammered.

'I think you do. You've been operating illegally for years, haven't you?'

He moved swiftly and grabbed Carl's sweater.

'Now you listen. Get your sorry self out of here and don't come back or I'll have every detective in South Africa on to you faster than you can blink.'

He shoved Carl out through the front door.

'Oh, and one other thing. I'll be adopting the child whether you like it or not. Just remember that when the time comes. I have no need to remind you that it will be in your interests to co-operate.'

Carl scurried down the path to his car.

'I'll take you all to court,' he yelled. 'I have friends in high places. You haven't heard the last of this.'

Joel shut the door firmly. His grin faded when he noticed that Julia was trembling from head to foot.

She demanded furiously, 'Just what was all that about you contacting my ex-husband by telephone? I wondered how Carl knew where to find us, and now it all becomes clear. You're the one who told him!'

'I don't deny it,' Joel said calmly.

'Why did you do it? Haven't you interfered in our lives enough?'

'It may look like that from your point of view, but I had my reasons.'

'And just what were those reasons?'

'I don't think you are ready to hear them.'

'Try me.'

He hesitated.

'Look, we'll make a deal. Come back to South Africa with me and when the time is right I'll tell you everything.'

'What kind of an answer is that?'

'Look at it this way,' he reasoned quietly. 'It will be the answer to your immediate accommodation problem and at the same time provide you both with a pleasant holiday. The warmth will do wonders for Meggie. If she doesn't improve, we'll take her to a paediatrician. It will also get Carl Thornton off your back for the moment, give us both the opportunity to see which way he'll really jump.'

The warmth in his eyes enfolded her.

'I guarantee that when you eventually return to Scotland, you'll be a different woman, in more ways than one,' he added mysteriously.

Julia knew she was beaten. She'd already ditched her pride, for the time being, at any rate. Meggie was the important consideration here, and put like that, she had nothing to lose. Suddenly she remembered the small prayer she'd uttered on Sunday. Perhaps this was the corner she'd asked God to back her into so she'd know which way to turn. Certainly there appeared to be no other course open to her at this point.

'I'll come,' she agreed.

Joel closed his eyes and released the breath he hadn't realised he'd been holding. Once Julia had experienced life at Dusty Plains she wouldn't want to live anywhere else, he was certain of it. He'd have the time and opportunity to show her how much he loved her. And then there was the little matter of the diamond.

'Great,' he said casually. 'I think this calls for a cup of coffee.'

7

Marta, Joel's housekeeper, received the news of their impending arrival with commendable calm. She bullied Dora, the housemaid, into putting on a clean uniform and instructed Magda to remove the lamb cutlets from the freezer.

'Casserole,' she informed the scullery maid in their own language. 'The master shall have my lamb casserole tonight.'

The remainder of the day was spent cleaning windows and polishing furniture with scant opportunity for unimportant things such as lunch breaks! By the time Joel's estate car was seen purring up the long drive at five-thirty, even Target, the black Labrador, was all fired up. He ran out to greet them, barking excitedly.

When she saw him, Meggie, staring

wearily through the car window after the long drive, perked up considerably. She had taken to calling Joel Daddy, and nothing would convince her otherwise, much to Julia's discomfort. Joel, on the other hand, appeared to see nothing unusual in the situation.

'Is that your dog, Daddy?' Meggie asked as he helped her from the car.

'Yes, that's Target,' he replied easily, turning to pat the dog. 'Target, this is Miss Meggie Thornton. I'll expect you to guard her well, old man. And remember to play gently with the little lady.'

Unable to keep the note of pride from his voice he smiled at Julia.

'Welcome to Dusty Plains.'

Julia gazed about her in awe. She'd never seen anything like it. The magnificent landscape stretched in every direction as far as the eye could see, with sheep dotted across the vast, semi-arid plains in their thousands. She turned her gaze upon Joel's home and swallowed. It was extremely impressive.

The whitewashed building in the Cape Dutch style complete with its vine-covered veranda, gabled roof and large, blinking, timber-framed windows looked back at her, rosily serene in the afternoon sunshine.

'It's wonderful,' she murmured huskily.

How fortunate Joel was to live here. No wonder he was so pleased to be back. A uniformed young African man arrived to carry in their suitcases. He greeted Joel warmly and cast covert glances in Julia's direction before launching into a long, welcome speech in his own language. Joel clapped him on the back, replied in kind, and ushered Julia and Meggie into the house where Marta was waiting to receive them, wearing one of her rare smiles. The housekeeper took one look at Meggie and was lost.

Joel, watching her, gave an exaggerated sigh of relief.

'You have a new ewe-lamb to watch over now, Marta,' he mocked. 'See to it that you don't spoil her.'

'No, sir,' Marta agreed blandly.

The child would have the best of what Dusty Plains had to offer, she determined privately, and as for the young child's mother, anyone could see that the master was besotted. Her prayers had at last been answered. A mistress is exactly what Dusty Plains needed.

Dora, resplendent in her clean overall, proudly showed Julia and Meggie to their bedrooms. In her broken English and with many signs, she offered them hot baths and glasses of orange juice. After the dust and heat of the journey, Julia was only to ready to agree. It was strange to suddenly find it was mid-summer.

Joel went to his quarters at the other end of the long passage and emerged half an hour later with his thick, dark hair still damp from the shower. Julia's breath caught at the sight of him in a clean pair of jeans which moulded his strong thighs like a second skin. Her adrenaline surged even further at the sight of the dark sweater stretched over his powerful chest, its sleeves pushed up to reveal bronzed forearms and an expensive gold watch. He looked rock solid, reliable and completely at ease, with an aura of authority which was wholly male — a man who was very definitely the master of his own domain.

What Julia was beginning to realise was that there was more to him than she'd thought. He was an honourable man. Comparisons were said to be odious, but no man could have been more different from Carl. At the memory of Meggie's father her heart lurched in fear. Surely he wouldn't follow them here to this desolate paradise in the depths of Africa. A moment later she dismissed the thought as ludicrous. Joel was here. He would protect her and Meggie. The thought made her feel utterly secure.

'We'll have a quiet drink before

dinner,' Joel suggested easily, instructing Marta to bring Meggie a glass of lemonade.

He ushered them into the conservatory where they sat and watched the sunset painting brilliant colours across the evening sky.

'It's very isolated here,' Julia ventured.

'Yes. There's a harsh, lonely beauty about the place which works its incredible magic on even the most shallow of personalities.'

'Are you never lonely?' she enquired curiously.

'I am at times,' he admitted, 'but one gets so used to the peace and quiet that an extended trip into civilisation soon palls, believe me.'

She didn't quite dare to question him further about his social life. He was a virile man and must surely enjoy the company of women, but that was not exactly her business.

'I have plenty of friends in Hopeford,' Joel continued easily. 'If I feel like socialising, it's a forty-minute drive by car. If I'm in a hurry, I fly. The farm has a small plane. Both Piet and I have a pilot's license, and Piet takes Anna into Kimberley quite often, to shop.'

'Piet?'

'The farm manager and his wife. You'll meet them. Anna's expecting her second child soon, and they have a son, Davey, who has just started school in Hopeford. Piet drives him in every morning, but I daresay he'll become a weekly boarder when he's older. At the moment it's the summer holiday, so he's at home. Meggie will be pleased to have someone to play with.'

Meggie was more than pleased. Within a week Davey Driemeyer had become her friend, protector and hero. The two were inseparable, so much so that Julia began to worry what would happen when the time came for her and Meggie to leave. After such a wonderful holiday, it would be difficult to return to normal living.

Meggie's cough had all but disappeared. She played outside for most of the day and soon grew tanned and healthy. Julia could scarcely believe she was the same child. Her appetite had always been good, but now she was eating them out of house and home, much to Marta's delight.

Joel, watching Meggie chase after a ball with Trigger and Davey, observed with all the pride of a father, 'She's cute, isn't she? Is this the same little girl I met just six weeks ago, I wonder.'

'She's improved greatly,' Julia acknowledged. 'Thank you, Joel. You've given us a wonderful time. It's going to be difficult to leave.'

'There's no hurry,' he assured her smoothly. 'Stay as long as you like.'

'That's very kind of you but I'd like to be back in Scotland by about the end of January, and it's the twentieth already. I've been meaning to phone the airlines to see if I can get a flight.'

Her eyes became shadowed.

'I have to find some accommodation

for us both, and a job. I'm thinking of moving to a remote spot somewhere on the West coast of Scotland.'

It was a prospect which filled her with secret dread, but she went on brightly.

'I've quite made up my mind.'

She'd spent most of the previous night making plans, deciding to revert to her maiden name. She would henceforth be known as Julia Rose MacGregor, and Meggie would be Meggie MacGregor. It would mean cutting themselves off from the rest of the family but if they could lie low for a year or two, maybe Carl would forget all about them.

'May I ask you something?' Julia blurted. 'You promised we'd . . . well, discuss things once we were here at Dusty Plains.'

Joel gave an inward sigh. He knew what was coming and couldn't put her off for much longer.

'Certainly. Fire away.'

'I need to know why you contacted

Carl in the first place. If you hadn't done so, he'd never have found me and come up with that disgraceful scheme to extort money from you. I don't believe for one moment that he genuinely wants Meggie, and as for that Leandra women, they aren't even married!'

'I couldn't agree more.'

'Then why? Why did you phone him?'

Oh, sweetheart, Joel thought, if only you knew. The trouble is, you're not ready to hear it. He cleared his throat and spoke blandly.

'I telephoned him to tell him I'd be marrying you and that I wished to have custody of Meggie.'

Julia gave a startled gasp, which he ignored.

'Unfortunately, Carl thought he could use that knowledge to make me pay up. As you've rightly said, he doesn't really want Meggie but guessed we'd do anything to keep her. So he flew to Scotland to find you after I'd

141

inadvertently given away your where-abouts. That first visit and all the hogwash about his wife wanting a baby was just a ground-laying exercise for his next little scheme to make me pay up and adopt Meggie for a fee. I'm afraid to say I did the unforgivable. I underestimated the enemy.'

Julia's gaze fastened on him for a long moment.

'Why would you say that you wanted to marry me?'

A gleam entered his eyes.

'You tell me.'

She shrugged flippantly.

'How can I, a mere female, determine the workings of a man's mind?'

Joel's lips twitched.

'Then don't try.'

Julia went to bed that night all the more determined to leave Dusty Plains by the end of the month. Joel's attraction for her was growing stronger by the day. He was the most considerate man she'd ever met. He was also sensitive, caring and strong. If she wasn't careful she'd sink into those muddy waters they called love — and promptly drown.

Joel seemed preoccupied at breakfast. He informed them that he would be flying into Kimberley and regretted that he couldn't offer to take them.

'Business,' he said firmly. 'I'll be back in time for dinner.'

Julia watched the plane take off from the airstrip, feeling unaccountably lonely. She busied herself pottering around the garden for an hour while Meggie played at the Driemeyers' with Davey.

Just before lunch Julia decided to walk over the hill and fetch her, as it would be an excellent opportunity to meet Davey's mother. The Driemeyers' house was one befitting a farm manager, not nearly as magnificent as Joel's but large and rambling with a neat garden and stabling for the two ponies which grazed in the adjoining paddock. Anna was in the garden, wearing a large sunhat as she went about dead-heading the roses. Within two minutes of meeting her, Julia knew she'd found a friend.

'I've been longing to meet you,' Anna confided, 'but with this baby almost due I hesitated to walk so far, and Piet's been too busy to drive me over. Your little girl is gorgeous, isn't she? She's quite won Davey's heart. I hope we have a girl this time. I'd like one just like Meggie.'

'Davey is special, too,' Julia assured her warmly. 'Meggie is going to miss him when we go.'

Anna looked surprised.

'I thought . . . I didn't realise . . . '

She stopped, embarrassed.

'The thing is, I understood that you were engaged to Joel. It's probably just servants' talk. I'm sorry, I didn't mean to pry.'

'No problem.'

Julia shrugged, hiding her consternation. Where had Anna got that impression? It's not as though she and Joel were constantly locked together in public embrace! The very thought of being in his arms made her heart leap in her chest. He was such an exciting man. Any woman would want to be loved by him. It was just as well she was not any woman.

'Meggie and I will be leaving in about ten days' time,' she said quickly.

'I see. In that case,' Anna said brightly, 'won't you and Joel come to a barbecue on Saturday evening? We'll invite a few friends from Hopeford. It's time we had a bit of a shindig again. After the baby's here I'll be out of commission for a bit. Do say you'll come.'

Julia took Meggie home for lunch. The longer she stayed at Dusty Plains, the more she loved it and the harder it would be to leave. But leave, she must. Soon!

Joel joined her for their evening drink in the conservatory. His gaze flicked over her with a hungry gleam in their depths. Only one day apart, and he'd missed her terribly. This was becoming harder and harder.

'Julia.'

'Yes?'

She looked up, arrested by something in his voice.

'I've found you a job.'

She blinked.

'What do you mean, a job? I can't stay here. I'm leaving soon.'

'Well, why not reconsider? You could stay on for a few more months without having to concern yourself about things like accommodation or employment back home. And you certainly would not be required to hide yourself away from your ex-husband.'

It sounded tempting, but she knew she should get away. Her resistance to Joel's charm was crumbling fast.

'What kind of a job?' she asked, in spite of herself.

'Writing children's books.'

Julia almost dropped her glass.

'Who told you I write?'

He grinned.

'I saw your books on Aunt Jemima's

bookshelf and read them all. You're good, Julia. I spoke to my publisher today and he bought the idea straight away. You are being asked to write a series on children in South African history, factual stories, or fiction based on fact. It'll involve a bit of research, of course.'

'Which children?'

'Oh, the popular tale of little Rachel De Beer who gave her life for her younger brother, or young Dirkie Uys who aided his father so bravely on the battlefield whilst fighting the Zulus, that sort of thing. Maybe even the story of the siege of Kimberley as told through the eyes of a child. The subject is limitless. How does it all grab you?'

Julia's eyes were shining. It was like a dream come true.

'You mean, I'll be able to write full time?'

'Why not? You can stay here until the assignment is finished, and Meggie can go to school with Davey. Take as much time as you like. My publisher assures me that every school library in the country will take these books. You'll make yourself a packet. Then you can return to Scotland, should you wish to do so.'

Julia struggled with herself for all of two seconds. Joel had just offered her the chance she'd wanted all her life, and all other considerations faded into insignificance.

'I'll do it,' she said and laughed, feeling like a puppy with two tails.

Joel hid his relief behind an inscrutable mask. The longer he could keep her at Dusty Plains, the easier things would be.

On Friday Meggie spent the day with the Driemeyers while Joel flew Julia to Kimberley to meet the publisher, Mr Adams. Afterwards they visited the Mine Museum and retraced the lives of the rough and ready diggers during the heady days of the diamond rush. Julia gazed through the glass at the first officially-recorded diamond discovered in the country, the Eureka, and appeared to be totally fascinated. It was all Joel could do to remain silent about the secret he carried.

The Big Hole itself was an astonishing sight, being the largest hand-dug excavation in the world. Julia found herself fantasising about writing a story concerning a diamond find. Maybe she could include something like that in her series. A young girl, perhaps, who finds a diamond whilst walking along the banks of the Orange River.

She told Joel about it, only to wonder at his reaction.

He gazed at her for a long time and finally said in a curious voice, 'What a good idea.'

They dined at the Eureka Hotel before visiting a few more places of historic interest. Finally they returned to the plane. It had been one of the most exhilarating days Julia could ever remember. To be honest, it was the company of the man beside her in the cockpit which had provided the glitter. She didn't need any gemstones for that!

When they landed at the homestead, Julia climbed down from the aircraft feeling overcome by a mixture of consternation and despair. The shocking fact was that she had fallen deeply in love with Joel Mortimer.

8

Anna Driemeyer telephoned Julia after dinner to say that the barbecue was arranged for the next evening.

'That's great, Anna. Is there anything I can do?' Julia asked.

Soon she was engrossed in their plans, thankfully able to shelve the disturbing thoughts which had been plaguing her ever since she'd recognised her feelings. The unwelcome discovery that she loved Joel was like a knife in an old wound. How had she allowed herself to be so foolish? She'd promised herself that she would never love again. Once she'd realised the strong attraction Joel had for her, she should have taken stronger measures to dispel it.

It would make things doubly awkward now that she was committed to remaining at Dusty Plains for at least the next six months. Her only hope was to avoid Joel as much as possible, starting now! After dinner Julia refused to take coffee with him in the living-room.

'I'm going to my room to read,' she told him abruptly.

Joel's gaze narrowed thoughtfully. She'd been keen to watch a television documentary on the Kruger National Park, a fact of which he reminded her.

'I've changed my mind,' Julia mumbled, and fled down the passage.

Her new discovery was destroying her poise. She was so unsteady, her knees felt drunk.

Joel took his coffee out on to the veranda in order to enjoy the summer evening, wondering what had happened to make Julia change her mind. Mingled with his exasperation was the happy knowledge that Julia was not as immune to him as she liked to appear. He'd seen it in her eyes today. It was early days yet and he would need to give her time, not easy.

Next evening, the delicious aroma of roasting meat assailed them as they approached the Driemeyers' home. It was a glorious evening. Julia and Joel walked with an excited Meggie dancing between them.

'Davey's mother is going to have a baby,' she announced importantly. 'Can we have one, too?'

Julia's face went as pink as her cotton top.

'I'm afraid that is out of the question, Meggie.'

'Why?'

'Well, it's just not possible.'

'Why is it out of the question?' Meggie persisted.

Julia darted Joel a helpless glance.

'Well, it's not that easy. I'll explain it to you later.'

Beside her Joel gave a snort which sounded suspiciously like a laugh.

'Coward,' he mocked softly.

Half a dozen people were gathered around the fires, sipping drinks as they chatted. Julia glanced around in time to see Meggie take Davey's hand and run off to play. Piet Driemeyer offered to fetch their drinks while Anna made the introductions.

'Joel, you've met Rupert Penright from Hopeford? Harley Penright's son.'

Joel shook the other man's hand, hiding his dislike.

'Indeed. Evening, Penright. May I introduce Mrs Julia Thornton?'

Rupert Penright looked down his nose at Julia. An indiscreet young man with an inflated opinion of his own importance, he greeted her in what she considered to be an off-hand fashion and proceeded to give her the once-over from sly blue eyes before shooting Joel a cunning glance.

'Taken your grandfather's instructions to heart, I see,' he sneered.

Joel ignored him.

'How is your father?' he asked politely.

Rupert snorted.

'Still as old-fashioned as ever. About time he retired! One of these days I'll be taking over the family firm as senior partner and then we'll see some changes, believe me. Harley's too sentimental. When I'm in charge . . . '

He droned on smugly about his own capabilities.

'Another drink?' Joel eventually suggested, keen to interrupt.

He disappeared with their glasses.

'Lovely evening,' Julia observed, equally keen to change the subject.

Rupert was the most self-absorbed male she'd met in a long time, since Carl, in fact. He ignored her comment, his eyes like slits.

'Where did Joel find you?' he demanded haughtily. 'You're Scottish, aren't you? That figures.'

'What figures?'

He laughed.

'You mean to say you have no idea? Wise up, woman. Joel Mortimer is forced to marry a Scotswoman. Terms of his grandfather's will. Marry a Scot within the year or lose Dusty Plains. So when's the wedding?'

Julia felt the ground tilt beneath her.

'I beg your pardon?' she repeated, feeling quite sick.

It was all clear to her now. So Joel had been serious when he'd told Carl he wished to marry her and adopt Meggie, but only in order to safeguard an inheritance. He was no better than her first husband! Thanks to Rupert Penright she had discovered his scheme in time. Joel returned with their drinks. He handed Rupert a glass and shepherded Julia away, his face grim.

'You're upset, Julia. What has that obnoxious jerk been saying?'

Julia smiled sweetly.

'Obnoxious jerk? Oh, I wouldn't say that. He's rather nice. He warned me off you.'

Joel went very still.

'Explain that remark.'

'I have no intention of doing so,' Julia spat out. 'In my book you're the jerk, Joel Mortimer.'

She marched away to help Anna with the salads.

'Julia!'

Joel caught up with her and grabbed her arm, but she shook him off.

'Don't touch me! Confine your attentions to the steak instead.'

She was still shaking with anger by the time the meal was served. Julia filled her plate and Meggie's and went to sit with Anna and Piet, ignoring Joel's grim glances. She couldn't wait for the evening to end. For the next hour she chatted brightly with the other guests, but as soon as she could, she thanked the Driemeyers for their hospitality and went to find Meggie. Joel appeared beside her.

'Ready to go?' he asked.

'Yes.'

They returned home in silence with a sleepy Meggie marching between them. Julia put the child to bed and returned to her bedroom, only to find Joel waiting for her in the corridor.

'We are going to have a talk,' he said firmly.

Julia looked up at his determined

face and shrugged. The sooner they got it over with, the better.

'Fine by me.'

She preceded him into the study and looked around curiously. So this is where he wrote all those history books! Joel offered her a leather armchair, but Julia declined. What she had to say would not take long and she preferred to remain standing. Joel leaned against the desk and folded his arms across his chest, his eyes never leaving her face. Julia's hair had loosened completely from its braid and her heightened colour served to make her eyes all the brighter. He had never seen her looking more beautiful.

'You look very lovely,' Joel told her huskily.

Julia's lips tightened.

'Thank you, but there is no need to flatter me.'

Genuine astonishment flashed across his face.

'Why would I wish to do that?'

'Don't play games with me,' Julia

snapped. 'Let's get everything out in the open, shall we? You're getting ready to ask me to marry you, so you tell me I'm beautiful. It won't wash.'

Joel's eyes blazed with something she could not quite define.

'I see.'

He sounded indifferent and she felt snubbed.

'It's true, isn't it? You do want to marry me.'

'If you say so.'

'I know all about your grandfather's instructions to marry a Scotswoman, Joel, so allow me to save you the trouble of asking. I will not marry you, and I'm going back to Scotland as soon as I can arrange it.'

Not a muscle on his face moved.

'What about your contract with Adams? You want to write those books, don't you?'

'I can work from Scotland. I can do the research there. We have libraries and archives and the internet, too, you know!'

Joel's jaw clenched. His monumental patience with this beautiful, complex woman was almost at an end.

'I don't doubt it,' he reasoned calmly, 'but it would be a lot easier this end. I'd be on hand to help. My library is at your disposal. I could take you around the country.'

Julia shook her head so hard the glossy dark strands of hair whirled about her shoulders.

'No, thank you.'

'Then I shall have to change your mind for you.'

He took her into his arms and brought his lips down on hers in a fierce, punishing kiss. Julia, her emotions spiralling out of control, kissed him back with instinctive, mindless abandon. It wasn't what she'd planned to do at all, but it would give her something to take away with and remember. Joel lifted his head and wrapped his arms about her soft, trembling frame.

'Julia.'

'Yes?'

His deep voice turned husky.

'Marry me, please,' he said gently and pleadingly.

Julia's sanity returned in a rush.

'Are you deaf? I will not marry you. I will not be used!'

'Used? Where did you get that crazy idea? I would never hurt you. I love you. I've loved you from that moment I saw you.'

'No. You love this farm. Rupert Penright told me everything. Marry within the year and you will safeguard your inheritance, isn't that so? Isn't it?' she demanded shrilly.

Joel went white beneath his tan.

'I don't deny that fact.'

'Goodbye, Joel,' Julia cried, and ran from the room.

★   ★   ★

Meggie was distraught to find that her mother had booked their air tickets back to Scotland. She refused to eat her lunch and threatened to go and live at Davey's house.

'I want to stay in South Africa, Mummy,' she wailed. 'What about Target? We can't leave Target behind.'

'Target belongs here. I'll buy you a new puppy when we're settled.'

'I don't want a new puppy, I want Target. I want to stay here!'

Julia tried to reason with her.

'We don't belong here, Meggie. We belong in Scotland.'

'No, we don't! We belong at Dusty Plains!'

Joel, who had been listening from the doorway, cleared his throat.

'Out of the mouth of babes,' he muttered.

Julia whipped around.

'You've done enough damage already!'

Meggie flung herself at Joel, sobbing. Wordlessly he picked her up and gave her a hug.

'Let's go and see what Marta is baking in the kitchen,' he suggested brightly and carried her out.

Julia sighed. It was an impossible situation. She hadn't quite bargained for Meggie's stubborn streak to appear at this precise moment. The child would just have to accept that they were flying out in two days' time.

Despite Marta's roast beef and apricot flan, Meggie refused her dinner. She performed like a banshee when told to have her bath and hurled herself, still sobbing, into her bed.

By the time their last evening arrived Julia was at her wits' end. The sweet, reasonable, happy child of late had been replaced by an awkward, disobedient little fiend. The sooner tomorrow came and they could get on that aircraft, the better. She wandered out on to the veranda before going to bed. It would be pleasant to savour for one last time the night noises, the cool breezes off the plains and the beautiful starry skies. Joel appeared behind her.

'I have something to say to you, Julia,' he clipped.

Julia jumped.

'Say it, then,' she said and her heart twisted painfully.

'Come into the study.'

'Very well. I hope it won't take long. I'll give you all of two minutes.'

It was the second time she'd been into the room with its book-lined walls and leather furniture.

'Please, sit down.'

Despite herself, Julia watched curiously from the leather armchair as he went to a bookshelf, removed some of the books and activated the combination lock on what appeared to be a small safe. He put a hand into it and retrieved some documents together with a small black velvet pouch. Joel relocked the safe, turned around with an expressionless face and tossed the items onto her lap.

'These belong to you.'

Julia's eyes widened.

'I don't understand. What is it?'

'Take a look.'

The pouch had a drawstring top

which Julia quickly opened.

'It's a piece of glass.'

He smiled humourlessly.

'Very expensive glass. It's the Mortimer Diamond, Julia.'

'Diamond?' Julia gaped. 'You mean, it's an uncut gem?'

'You would need to have it properly cut and set, or you could sell it, whatever. That's your decision. You're a rich woman now, my dear.'

She stared uncomprehendingly at the papers.

'But it's worth a fortune! Why are you giving this to me? You must surely know that I cannot accept it. I suppose you're trying to bribe me into marrying you!'

Joel looked as though she'd hit him.

'Take your diamond,' he grated, 'and go.'

Julia jumped up.

'I don't know what this is all about, but one thing I do know — I won't accept charity, particularly from you!'

Joel went white.

'It is not charity,' he roared. 'It belongs to you, you stupid woman.'

There appeared to be something she was missing here. She stared into his furious face and decided to back down.

'I think you had better explain,' she said quietly.

Joel smiled nastily.

'Ah, so the lady has decided to listen, at last.'

9

Julia leaned back in her plane seat and closed her eyes, trying to ignore Meggie's mutinous, tear-stained face next to her. The scene at the airport had been beyond belief, and for the first time Julia had really questioned the wisdom of her decision to leave Dusty Plains.

'We have to leave, baby,' she murmured. 'It's for the best.'

Even to herself the words sounded hollow.

The air hostess, noting Meggie's distress, produced a little package containing a colouring book, crayons and one or two puzzles, which helped to ease the situation slightly. Nevertheless, Julia was alarmed to notice a new pallor under Meggie's tan. It would take some time for her to adjust to the sad fact that Joel Mortimer would not become her new daddy.

Aunt Jemima was watching from the window as their taxi drew up outside the large, sandstone house. By the time Julia and Meggie had been helped inside with their luggage, the driver paid and tea made, the old lady could not contain her curiosity a moment longer.

'There are some new books and toys on your bed, Meggie,' she coaxed. 'Why not go upstairs and take a look?'

'All right,' Meggie agreed in a subdued voice, 'but I'd much rather be at Dusty Plains playing with Davey and Target.'

'Yes, well, perhaps you will have the good fortune to return before long, for another holiday. Now run along, there's a dear.'

As soon as the child had departed the old lady turned to her niece.

'You had better tell me what is going on, Julia.'

Julia sighed.

'I'm in such a muddle myself, I hardly know.'

'Start at the beginning. What is all this you mentioned on the phone about a diamond?'

Julia poured herself another cup of tea before replying.

'Well, Seth Mortimer, Joel's grandfather, revealed on his deathbed that there was this family diamond. Joel didn't know anything about it. When he finally discovered where it was he found that it was so impressive, he went to the archives to research its history. Apparently it was quite a find at the time, being one of the earliest gems discovered on the banks of the Orange River in South Africa.'

'Go on.'

'The diamond was discovered by a young Scots woman who was employed as a governess to a wealthy Victorian family who had emigrated there. She was taking a walk one day and found what she thought was a pretty piece of glass. When she showed it to a young man she'd met, he told her it was a diamond, and he offered to take it and have it valued for her, which he did. He then informed her falsely that the stone was inferior and almost worthless, much to her disappointment. The young man also told a pack of lies to discredit her with her employers so that she would be dismissed. She had to return to Scotland where she supposedly lived in poverty when in fact she could have been a very wealthy woman.'

'How sad. Did she ever query the young man's story about the diamond being worthless?'

'Apparently not. She was a simple, naïve lass from Perthshire who believed that everyone spoke the truth, as she did.'

'Poor girl. I wonder who she was.'

Julia grinned.

'Her name was Julia Rose Buchanan and far from living in poverty, she married James Edward MacGregor who owned an estate near Gleneagles, Perthshire. He was my great, great grandfather, Aunt Jemima.'

'Good gracious, dear girl. Joel discovered all that?'

'And more,' Julia said, her grin widening. 'That unscrupulous young man who conned her was none other than a Mortimer. His guilty conscience drove him to confess his misdeeds to his father, who forbade that the diamond be sold until they could find the girl and return it. He wished to restore the honour of the Mortimer family name but by this time, of course, Julia Rose had disappeared and couldn't be traced. So the diamond was kept in a safe and passed on to future generations until Seth's late wife, Elizabeth, hit on the idea of returning it to a Scots girl, any Scots girl, just to be rid of the thing.'

'Hm,' Aunt Jemima murmured.

'On his deathbed, Seth Mortimer urged Joel to marry a Scots girl, which would keep the diamond in the family and at the same time right the injustice done all those years ago. The bride was to be presented with the diamond on her wedding day.'

'A sensible idea, it seems to me.'

Aunt Jemima, who hadn't previously known the details Julia had just revealed but was certainly privy to Joel's thoughts on marriage, ventured to voice her next question.

'Has Joel decided who the girl is to be?'

'Oh, yes. Me!'

The sad mouth alerted Aunt Jemima to the fact that Julia was not the delighted bride-to-be she had been expecting.

'Well?'

'I turned him down,' she retorted defensively. 'Oh, Aunt, Seth's will stipulated that he marry within the year or the farm would be sold. Joel only wished to marry me in order to keep the darned place.'

'I disagree,' Aunt Jemima contradicted. 'It seems to me that Joel asked you to marry him not to save his own hide, but yours.'

'Nonsense. How can you say that?'

'I can say it because I know for a fact that he loves you. Only a man in love would desire the best for his woman. Joel wanted you to have the diamond despite the fact that you turned down his proposal of marriage. If he'd been unscrupulous he could have sold the gem and then bought back the farm anyway, were he so keen to keep it. Instead, he wanted you to be financially secure, and in so doing, he is prepared to lose everything. But then, he's an honourable man. He'd never stoop to deceit of any description. You've misjudged the man badly, Julia.'

Far from looked chastened, Julia laughed.

'No, I haven't misjudged him. I realised all this for myself, the night before I left.'

'I'm pleased to hear it. So what are you going to do about it?'

'I've already done it. I'm not without my own sense of honour. Do you think I could stand by and watch a man like that lose the home he loves?'

'I don't understand. If you aren't going to marry him, how do you propose to save Joel's skin?'

'I've already done it, Aunt,' Julia replied. 'I left the diamond on his desk.'

★   ★   ★

Joel returned from the airport in a foul mood. Julia was the most frustrating woman he'd ever had the misfortune to meet, let alone love. She couldn't see further than her very beautiful little nose. Didn't she realise that marrying him would solve all her problems? And as for Meggie, leaving her at the airport had almost broken his heart.

He roared up the drive at Dusty Plains. Marta, looking out of the window with a long face, was moved to scold the hapless gardener who had just at that moment appeared at the back door.

'Well?' she snapped. 'What are you standing there for, Lucas? Get the hosepipe out! Can't you see the master's car will be filthy?'

Joel ate his dinner in morose silence that evening. Marta, darting him concerned little glances, informed the scullery maid that she didn't know what the world was coming to. Master Joel was the best catch in South Africa and yet the young lady had chosen to leave him.

Joel's publisher had furnished him with a deadline and he was already behind schedule. He decided there was nothing for it but to resume work as soon as possible, if he could concentrate. All he could see in his mind's eye was a tearful, little Meggie and a stubborn, white-faced Julia as they boarded the flight. He gulped down the last of his coffee and took himself into the study. It was going to be a very long evening.

He sat down at his desk and stared uncomprehendingly at the black velvet pouch before him. He gazed at it for a very long time before snatching it up and emptying its contents onto the palm of his hand. What on earth was the Mortimer Diamond doing here? Then he spotted the plain envelope with his name on it, tore it open and scanned Julia's note.

Dear Joel, I cannot accept this. I am giving it back to the Mortimer family, to be used as you wish. I hope it will comfort you in some measure when you lose Dusty Plains. I am sorry I cannot marry you. You are a fine, wonderful person and it may surprise you to know that despite everything, I did fall in love with you. I wish you all the happiness you deserve. Julia.

Joel re-read the note with his heart hammering and the blood roaring through his head. So he hadn't been wrong about her after all! Mrs Julia Thornton might be the most exasperating woman he knew, but she had finally admitted that she loved him, and that was all he needed to know! He locked the pouch in the safe, took a hasty shower and threw some clothing into a suitcase before leaving a note in the kitchen for Marta. Target, snug in his bed, cocked an enquiring ear and yawned.

'It's a boring life, Target,' Joel agreed happily. 'I'll be driving all the way back to the airport tonight and I'll darned well sit there on standby until I can find an airline which will take me.'

★ ★ ★

After breakfast Julia sat down at the kitchen table to work out her options. Her savings book revealed a very slim purse indeed. She did not wish to impose upon Aunt Jemima any longer than was absolutely necessary so it was imperative that she find work. Seeing that she intended to live somewhere on the west coast of Scotland it seemed obvious that she needed to begin looking in that area. The only trouble was, Meggie had awoken this morning with another fever. There was no way she could head off and leave Aunt Jemima burdened with a sick child.

It was worrying. Meggie had been exceptionally well for the entire time they were at Dusty Plains but the moment they'd returned she had become ill. It was only the middle of February and Scotland was still in the grip of icy weather, which did not bode well for Meggie's chest. As for Carl, she could only assume that he had gone back to Johannesburg. Joel had been reasonably sure they would not hear from him again and she fervently hoped he was right. Still, it would be wisdom to hide away for a while. It would be unthinkable to have him re-enter their lives at this stage.

'Why so glum, dear?' Aunt Jemima enquired.

Julia immediately summoned a bright smile.

'Oh, it's nothing, aunt. I'm just considering my future, that's all.'

Aunt Jemima nodded.

'And about time, too.'

Julia looked indignant.

'What do you mean? I've always been prudent when it comes to money.'

'I know, dear, but I'm talking about men.'

This was rich, Julia thought. Aunt Jemima had never even been married!

'What about them?' she demanded.

'Julia, may I be very straight with you?'

Julia hid a grin.

'When are you ever not forthright, my dear aunt?'

'Julia, dear, this is no laughing matter. When it comes to men, you are as dumb as a post. It's about time you realised that there are some men you can trust in this world. There are any amount of them, in fact.'

Julia sobered quickly.

'As a matter of fact, I agree with you.'

'You do? Then what's your problem?'

'I can't let go the pain of the past. I want to, but I lack the courage.'

Aunt Jemima nodded.

'Then you need to make up your mind to forgive and move on. You cannot cling to your misery, Julia. Don't give Carl that victory, or he'll sour the rest of your life. He'll destroy your future happiness. You're a lovely girl and you deserve to be happy. You deserve to be given the chance to make someone else happy, too. Don't deny yourself. Don't deny my godson, either. He deserves happiness as much as you do.'

'How,' Julia asked slowly, 'did you know I love Joel?'

'It's as plain as day.'

'It's too late, Aunt. He was quite glad to see the back of me. I was very rude, you know.'

'You obviously don't know Joel. Now, another cup of tea, dear?'

After lunch, Julia took Meggie's temperature and was relieved to find it had returned to normal. Still, it would be prudent to walk into the village for some medication in case she became ill during the night.

'I'm just going down to the chemist, Meggie,' she said. 'If you stay there at the window, you can see me walking home up the hill. I shan't be long.'

But Meggie was not listening. She was already at the window, her small eyes popping out of her head.

'There's my daddy,' she shrieked, hurling herself at the front door. 'He's come to take me home!'

Julia went rigid with shock.

'What?'

She watched, unable to move, as Joel came into the hall. He dumped his suitcase on the carpet and opened his arms wide. Meggie, like a small, flying monkey, leaped straight into them.

'I knew you'd come,' she shouted triumphantly. 'Can we go home now, please, and play with Target?'

'Not so fast.' Joel laughed. 'I've only just arrived. The man needs a cup of coffee, at least, and then there are presents to be opened.'

Meggie deposited a rather sloppy kiss on his chin.

'You are the best Daddy in the whole, wide world.'

Julia, standing quietly behind them, marvelled at the strong bond between her daughter and a man she'd only known for a few weeks. Children were so trusting. At that moment she wished she were a child. She took a deep breath.

'Hello, Joel,' she said shakily.

He looked up, his eyes inscrutable.

'Julia.'

Aunt Jemima bustled through from the kitchen.

'Oh, it's you. What took you so long?' she demanded. 'I thought you'd never get here. You look as though you could do with a good sleep, young man. I suppose you've been sitting about in airports for half the night.'

He grinned.

'And good afternoon to you, too. Coffee?'

'I'll make it,' Julia volunteered hastily, disappearing into the kitchen in order to compose herself.

She took her time about making the coffee, somehow reluctant to face him again. By the time she'd carried the tray into the living-room Meggie had happily disappeared into her room with the toys Joel had purchased en route and Aunt Jemima was sampling a chocolate from the box she'd just unwrapped. Joel had fallen fast asleep in an armchair. His strong features had softened in sleep, his dark hair was suitably untidy and his thick lashes were lying against his tanned cheeks, making tiny shadows on them. Aunt Jemima offered Julia a chocolate.

'In all the rush he even remembered to bring me my favourites,' she said, glancing fondly at her godson. 'Have one, Julia. They're rather dark and bitter on the outside, but — '

'I know,' Julia interrupted, 'there's a sweet, soft centre.'

She placed the tray on the sofa table. Aunt Jemima rose.

'No coffee for me, thank you, dear. I'm off to have my afternoon nap.'

Julia was left alone with the coffee tray and a sleeping giant, at a loss to know what to do. It seemed a pity to wake him. He was obviously exhausted. She was about to tiptoe past him when his hand snaked out and gripped her wrist. With a gasp she landed in his lap, her cheek pressed against him.

'There's nothing wrong with a dark, bitter outside,' Joel whispered, 'providing there is a sweet, soft centre. Do you have such a thing, Julia?'

His voice was low and vibrant, and she saw the fire in his eyes.

'I . . . ' she began, barely capable of coherent thought.

Joel's mouth had covered her own, and more than anything she wanted his kisses. She wanted to belong to him. This, at last, was a man she could trust. But did he still want her?

'Julia,' he murmured.

It wasn't easy keeping control of his impulses. The combination of fatigue and Julia Thornton was making him light-headed. He let her go and stood up.

'Coffee?' he prompted.

'Uh . . . sure.'

Julia smoothed her hair and lifted Aunt Jemima's silver pot with shaking hands. He took the cup and thanked her politely, draining it in one go.

'What is it with you women?' he observed wryly. 'You serve coffee in cups I can barely hold. I'm forever asking Marta to use a kitchen mug.'

'I'll fetch one,' Julia immediately offered.

'No. I'd rather you were back in my arms.'

He replaced the offending cup in its saucer and reached for Julia, grasping her firmly by the shoulders.

'Listen, Julia, because I'm not saying this twice. I'm taking you and Meggie back with me to Dusty Plains, so you'd better start packing. I love you now more than ever and I intend to make you my wife, and it's non-negotiable.'

Before Julia could attempt any sort of

reply he drew her closer.

'I offer you not only my love, but my total commitment. I want us to live and love in complete trust. I want us to have children together, if that's what you want. We'll grow old together at Dusty Plains and watch our grandchildren running about on the lawns.'

His eyes, red-rimmed with fatigue, were still flecked with silver as he searched her own.

'I want to adopt Meggie, not least because her father is likely to be put away for a very long time. He has been arrested.'

'Carl arrested?' Julia gasped.

'I heard it on the news. That scam I mentioned. He was already out on bail, actually, and offended again, so he won't stand much of a chance of getting off this time. The fraud was so considerable that he'll get fifteen to eighteen years, I reckon. He's been under investigation for some time. My buddy at the Ace Detective Agency has been keeping me informed.'

Julia let out a long, shuddering sigh.

'He can't bother us any more then. Meggie's safe.'

'Yes, and you are, too, my darling. Trust me.'

Julia gazed up at him with her heart in her eyes.

'Yes. I do. I love you, too. I've come to realise that love involves trust. I'm willing to risk my happiness and Meggie's with you, Joel.'

Joel felt humbled by the love of this beautiful woman. He would not let her down. He would not betray her as Carl had done.

'Thank you,' he said huskily.

'No, thank you,' Julia whispered.

One month later, Julia Rose MacGregor married Dr Joel Mortimer in the old stone church in Hopeford, South Africa, where, unbeknown to her, the other Julia Rose, her ancestor, had once worshipped.

Aunt Jemima was present, resplendent in her pink wedding hat. The twins, Ginny and Kirsty, were unable to attend but had made plans to fly out for their summer holidays with their respective husbands. Marta and the others had remained at Dusty Plains in order to ensure that the caterers from Hopeford did not put a foot wrong, because Master Joel and his new bride deserved only the very best.

The Driemeyers were also present, their family now increased with the recent safe arrival of little Susanna.

Julia Mortimer, nee MacGregor, swept radiantly down the aisle on her new husband's arm whilst Meggie, daintily clad in her blue party dress, darted past the other guests.

She arrived before anyone else on the front steps of the church and it was there that young Davey Driemeyer, hero, friend and protector, helped Meggie to throw her roses for the happy couple, her mummy and daddy!

We do hope that you have enjoyed reading this large print book.

Did you know that all of our titles are available for purchase?

We publish a wide range of high quality large print books including:
Romances, Mysteries, Classics
General Fiction
Non Fiction and Westerns

Special interest titles available in large print are:
The Little Oxford Dictionary
Music Book, Song Book
Hymn Book, Service Book

Also available from us courtesy of Oxford University Press:
Young Readers' Dictionary
(large print edition)
Young Readers' Thesaurus
(large print edition)

For further information or a free brochure, please contact us at:
Ulverscroft Large Print Books Ltd.,
The Green, Bradgate Road, Anstey,
Leicester, LE7 7FU, England.
Tel: (00 44) **0116 236 4325**
Fax: (00 44) **0116 234 0205**

Other titles in the
Linford Romance Library:

THREE TALL TAMARISKS

Christine Briscomb

Joanna Baxter flies from Sydney to run her parents' small farm in the Adelaide Hills while they recover from a road accident. But after crossing swords with Riley Kemp, life is anything but uneventful. Gradually she discovers that Riley's passionate nature and quirky sense of humour are capturing her emotions, but a magical day spent with him on the coast comes to an abrupt end when the elegant Greta intervenes. Did Riley love Greta after all?

SUMMER IN
HANOVER SQUARE

Charlotte Grey

The impoverished Margaret Lambart is suddenly flung into all the glitter of the Season in Regency London. Suspected by her godmother's nephew, the influential Marquis St. George, of being merely a common adventuress, she has, nevertheless, a brilliant success, and attracts the attentions of the young Duke of Oxford. However, when the Marquis discovers that Margaret is far from wanting a husband he finds he has to revise his estimate of her true worth.

CONFLICT OF HEARTS

Gillian Kaye

Somerset, at the end of World War I: Daniel Holley, unhappily married to an ailing wife and father of four grown-up children, is attracted to beautiful schoolteacher Harriet Bray, but he knows his love is hopeless. Daniel's only daughter, Amy, who dreams of becoming a milliner and is caught up in her love for young bank clerk John Tottle, looks on as the drama of Daniel and Harriet's fate and happiness gradually unfolds.

THE SOLDIER'S WOMAN

Freda M. Long

When Lieutenant Alain d'Albert was deserted by his girlfriend, a replacement was at hand in the shape of Christina Calvi, whose yearning for respectability through marriage did not quite coincide with her profession as a soldier's woman. Christina's obsessive love for Alain was not returned. The handsome hussar married an heiress and banished the soldier's woman from his life. But Christina was unswerving in the pursuit of her dream and Alain found his resistance weakening . . .

THE TENDER DECEPTION

Laura Rose

When Sophia Barton was taken from Curton Workhouse to be a scullery-maid at Perriman Court, her future looked bleak. Was it really an act of Providence that persuaded Lady Perriman to adopt her as her ward? Sophia was brought up together with the Perriman children, and before sailing with his regiment for India, George, the heir to the title, declared his love. But tragedy hit the family and Sophia found herself caught up in a web of mystery and intrigue.